Captain Cobwebb's Cowboys

Captain Cobwebb's Cowboys

Gordon Boshell

Illustrated by Graham Thompson

Armada

First published in 1969 by Chatto
& Windus. This edition first
published in Armada by Fontana
Paperbacks, 14 St. James's Place,
London SW1A 1PF.

© Gordon Boshell 1969

Printed in Great Britain
by Love & Malcomson Ltd.,
Brighton Road, Redhill,
Surrey.

(The illustration on page 6 is by the author)

CONTENTS

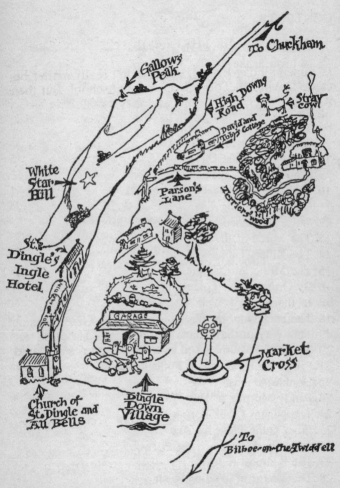

This is the village of Dingle Down, where David and Toby live. It was beyond Gallows Peak, in the weird forest behind White Star Hill, that they were ambushed at dead of night.

CHAPTER 1

WHAT CAME THROUGH THE WINDOW

It rained all day Friday, which didn't really matter because David and Toby Green were at school. But then it rained all Friday evening and they couldn't go out to play . . . at least, they could have done if Mrs Green had let them but she said 'No,' she said, 'I'm not going to have you catch your death of cold.' David said, 'But it's only wet: it's not cold.' And Mrs Green said, 'I didn't mean that kind of cold.' (Have you noticed that grown-ups so often don't say clearly what they do mean?) Anyway, that was that—as Mrs Green said, again not very clearly—and the two boys had to stay in.

On Saturday when they got up in the morning it was still raining and it rained all day and by late afternoon David and Toby began to run out of things to do: after all, you can't sit and read books *all* the time and it's difficult to think of any real games—boy-games, that is—that you can play indoors, especially with *two* grown-ups about the place, because Mr Green was at home all day on Saturdays and Sundays. He came out of his study and he looked over his spectacles at David and Toby and he said, '*Must* you run about yelling like Red Indians?'

'We *are* Red Indians,' said Toby. 'Wooolloowoolloowoolloowhooooooop!'

'And I'm going to scalp him,' said David. 'Woolloowoolloowoollowhoop!'

'Not with my potato-peeler you aren't,' cried Mrs Green, running in from the kitchen. 'Give that to me, I've been looking for it everywhere.'

'You don't play rough and rowdy games in the drawing-room,' said Mr Green—although he could see very well that they were doing just that.

'Give them an inch and they'll take a mile,' said Mrs Green.

'An inch of what?' asked Toby, who was two years younger than David and not quite as used to the queer things that grown-ups say.

'That will do, Toby,' replied Mrs Green severely. All this strange talk made Toby so baffled and exasperated that he wanted to cry. Being a boy, of course, he tried to stop himself doing so and he managed it pretty well except for one big sniff.

'Good heavens!' cried Mrs Green. 'He's starting a cold.'

'That means they'll both have one,' said Mr Green.

'They must go to bed at once,' said Mrs Green.

'A sound idea,' agreed Mr Green. 'Pyjamas, dressing-gowns, bed-socks, eiderdowns . . . lots of pillows. The boys can sit up in bed and read their books . . . quietly. Off you go . . .'

And it was no use arguing, David and Toby had to do as they were told.

Well, they sat up in bed and they tried to read, but they couldn't seem to get interested and finally Toby put his book down and said, 'Let's play *I Spy.*'

'Oh, all right,' said David. 'I spy with my little eye something beginning with C.'

'That's easy,' Toby said. 'I guessed it when I saw you look up at the ceiling. Right in the corner there . . . it's a cobweb.'

'You're right,' said David. And then he suddenly cried, 'Toby! Cobweb! Uncle Septimus! Adventure!'

And Toby said, 'Why, aren't we silly not to have remembered before now! Let's ask him, shall we?'

'You bet!' said David.

Most likely this conversation seems all nonsense to you, so it had better be explained. You see, there was a strange legend in the Green family about the boys' uncle, whose name was Septimus Cobwebb (he spelled it with two bs so as not to be confused with a spider cobweb).

It seems that one night, when he was a boy, Septimus

Cobwebb left a note to his father saying that he had gone out into the meadow where the fairies were supposed to dance and that he was going to sit in one of the dark green circles in the grass—the ones people call fairy rings—until the fairies appeared. Well, the fact is that Uncle Septimus never came back home, not ever again. But one day a strange woman in green knocked at the door of Grandfather Cobwebb's house and thrust a letter into his hand. It was from Uncle Septimus and it said he was well and happy but he was not coming back. But, it said, if ever any of the family needed help, they should write a message addressed to him care of The Four Winds, enclose a hair from their head and then set fire to the letter. Mr Green had once called on Uncle Septimus in this way to provide an adventure for David and Toby and it had really worked.*

In fact they had shown themselves so brave during this adventure that Uncle Septimus had given them a kind of private radio link directly with him. He had caused a magic blue mark to appear on each boy's right hand, at the bottom of the first finger.

'If you ever get bored, can't think of anything to do and want an adventure,' Uncle Septimus had said, 'all you have to do is to press that spot with the little finger of your left hand and speak your message.'

So now you know just what David and Toby were talking about.

'Have you put your finger properly, Toby?' asked David. 'Right. Now, one . . . two . . . three . . .' And they said, both together:

'This is David and Toby Green calling Uncle Septimus Cobwebb. Please will you make an adventure for us?'

Then they stopped and waited expectantly. Outside the rain still fell but the clouds had broken and a sudden great red ray of light from the setting sun blazed into the bedroom, almost blinding them.

* Told in *Captain Cobwebb*

9

'I wonder what's going to happen now?' whispered Toby.

Then David said suddenly, 'Ssh! Listen!!!!!!' (All those exclamation marks are to show how excited he was.)

'It's a horse . . .' said Toby.

'Galloping . . .' said David.

'Furiously,' cried Toby. 'And it's coming here!'

And indeed the pounding of steel-shod hooves was coming nearer and nearer at an astonishing rate. Soon the whole house seemed to be shaking.

'Run to the window,' David cried.

But before they could get their feet out of their beds, the galloping came to a stop with a great clatter of hooves. There was a sudden, strange kind of trumpeting, then a great whooshing noise. The window flew open . . . just for a second the light of the sun was blocked out and then . . .

SWISSH . . . BUMP . . . something, something hard and heavy, landed on the bedroom floor.

The whole room jumped. The beds seemed to dance up and down. And both David and Toby ducked their heads under the blankets, fearing that the ceiling must be about to fall in. There was a long silence.

Then a deep and rather drawly voice that seemed to come from somewhere down between the two beds said, 'Saay, hev I the honour of addressing David and Toby Green?'

CHAPTER 2

A LEAP IN THE DARK

'YES,' said David and Toby together. And Toby asked, 'Have you come from Uncle Septimus?' 'What kind of adventure shall we have this time?' said David. And they both turned in the direction of the voice.

What they saw then nearly made them hide their

heads under the blankets again. Just about on a level with their faces was a large cowboy hat and, from all around the wide rim of this hat, waves of blue smoke were rolling upwards. That was all they could see, for it was twilight now and the space between the beds was in deep shadow.

'He's on fire!' cried Toby.

'Off with the blankets and roll him in them,' said David briskly, because he knew this was the right thing to do if anybody's clothes caught fire. In a flash the two boys had ripped off a heavy blanket from each bed, flung it over the smoking hat and leaped from their beds to render first aid. But scarcely had their feet touched the carpet when two bony arms and two gaunt hands with a grip like steel shot out from under the blankets and held them powerless to move, while the drawly voice—a bit muffled this time—said, 'Well, I 'low pardner David and pardner Toby, yo' sure are quick on the draw. Howsomedever, pardners, there ain't no need to worry yo'selves none . . . see.' And with this the blankets were flung off and the cowboy hat pushed back off the head of its owner.

The two boys found themselves looking down on a completely bald head, very white, and underneath it a round face, of which only one feature was really clear—a little round button of a nose that was so close to the bowl of a tiny, short clay pipe that every time its owner drew on the pipe the nose reflected the red glow in the bowl like a beacon. Toby was so fascinated by the sight that he told David later he half expected the nose to turn green and amber as well, like the traffic lights.

In between the great puffs of blue smoke, the glow from the pipe showed something else. It showed that the cowboy—for it was a cowboy, as you're sure to have guessed already—was not lying down, or kneeling down, but actually standing up. He really must have been the smallest cowboy in the world because, even with the hat on, the top of the crown hardly came up to David's chin. He wore a leather waistcoat and a yellow and black checked shirt. Two enormous gleaming pistols hung from a wide leather belt full of bullets and beneath his leather trousers were high-heeled boots with great silver spurs.

Goodness knows how long they would have gone on gazing at the cowboy without saying anything if David had not remembered that it's very rude to stare at people, so he said, 'We're very glad to meet you, Mister . . . er . . .'

'Cassidy's the name, pardner,' drawled the cowboy. 'Lofty Cassidy . . .'

When he heard a name like this applied to such a little man Toby nearly choked himself trying not to laugh and David tried to help by slapping him hard on the back and saying, 'Is that better, Toby?' But Mr Cassidy—I mean Lofty Cassidy—wasn't deceived. He said, 'You go right ahead, pardner and hev a good laugh, if so be as you've a mind. Most folk does when they hears my name fer the fust time . . .'

'I'm terribly sorry, Mr Cassidy . . .' said Toby.

'Lofty,' the cowboy corrected him.

'Lofty,' said Toby. 'I wasn't laughing *at* you, you know.'

'Sure, I do,' answered the cowboy. 'Tain't no matter, think nothing of it. Guess I was made sorta concentrated—like that beef extract they talks about in the ad-ver-*tise*-ments—there ain't much of me but I'm powerful strong. Down at the Double C ranch—Double C stands for Cobwebb Cowboys—the boys reckon I'm *too* strong . . . thet's 'cause I keeps breakin' things.'

David was just opening his mouth to ask a question when Lofty Cassidy said, 'Now, pardners, it's getting dark and we hev to be off. But first: are you all set on havin' this adventure?'

'We sure are,' answered Toby, who had been listening closely to Lofty's way of talking and was beginning to pick it up.

'Ready to face any dangers?'

'Yes,' said both boys together.

'Boiling heat and freezing cold?'

'Yes.'

This is Lofty Cassidy, the world's smallest cowboy. Tobacco was his weakness and he used to say the next best thing to smoking the Pipe of Peace was to smoke his piece of pipe.

'Grizzly b'ars and rattlesnakes?'
'Yes.'
'Bad Men and Injuns?'
'Yes.'

'And you're willing to obey the rules drawn up by Captain Septimus Cobwebb, them being that once you pass the test and get started on the adventure, you won't never give in nor turn back but see it right through to the end. Even,' added Lofty Cassidy solemnly, 'if it means being shot or drowned?'

David said, 'Well, we can't expect to have adventures without taking risks, can we, Toby?'

And Toby said, 'I think when you start a thing you ought to see it through, don't you, David?'

'Sure thing,' said David (*he* was getting the habit now). 'So our answer is yes, Mr . . .'

'Lofty, pardner.'

'Sorry. The answer is yes, Lofty. And we're ready to take the test right now.'

There was a long silence. Lofty Cassidy hitched up his gun belt and turned to face the open window. It was dark outside, with the wind blowing a gale and a watery moon peering out now and again through scurrying black clouds.

'Now, pardners, listen ter me,' began Lofty. 'You stand behind me, Toby, and grab hold of my belt . . . Right? Now you, David, you got longer arms so you get close behind Toby, put 'em round him and grab hold o' my belt as well. You still sure you want to take this here test?'

'Yes.'

'Right. Then this is it . . . Fust I ses "Ready", then I ses "Go" . . . and when I ses "Go", we runs forward together, three steps towards that window—*and then we jumps*. Now . . . READY . . .'

'W-what, out of the w-w-w . . .?' Toby began. But it was far too late to ask any questions now, for Lofty had shouted 'GO' and they were rushing forward . . . They leaped from the bedroom floor and, with a wild yell of 'Yippeeee!' from Lofty Cassidy, and leaving a trail of sparks from his pipe behind them like a rocket, they found themselves outside the window and falling down, down, down in the howling darkness.

CHAPTER 3

THE AMAZING FOOT-WARMER

WELL, you know how it is when you find yourself falling . . . you want to cry out 'Ooooooo!' but you haven't enough breath to do it. David and Toby felt like that. They held on to Lofty's belt with all their strength as the three of them swooshed down through the air and then, ker-blump! they landed on something soft and yielding, their breath came back to them and I'm pretty certain that both the boys did *begin* to say 'Oh' (or perhaps 'Owww!') but if they did the sound was drowned by a terrific yell from Lofty.

'Yippee!' he cried. 'You sure passed that test with honours, pardners. Giddup, Fanty!' And, with a jingle of spurs and harness and a wild clatter of hooves, the three companions were carried off at a mad gallop.

The boys' minds were full of all kinds of questions, and while they are trying to sort out which question to ask first, there's perhaps time to tell you about the place where David and Toby live, when they're not off on an adventure, of course. Their village is called Dingle Down and as you'll see from the map on page 6, there's just one road that goes into it, from Bilboe-on-the-Twiddell, round the market square, past the church of St Dingle and All Bells and along to the St Dingle's Ingle Hotel. Here the Bilboe road changes its name to High Downs Road, and it runs along the foot of White Star Hill to two rather curious little villages called Chuckham and Chuckham-over-the-Water. There's a story about these villages but, right now, we'd better get back to David and Toby, because although Toby is still trying to decide which question to ask first, David has made up his mind.

'Lofty,' he asked, 'how could you be sure when we jumped out of the window that we'd land on your horse's back? You couldn't see him in the darkness.'

'Nope. Couldn't see him, pardner,' chuckled Lofty, 'but he could see me all right and get himself in the right place for us to land on his back. You see, Fanty ain't no common kinda hoss, he's . . .'

But Lofty didn't get any further because just then Toby burst out with his question. 'Where are we going, Lofty?'

'Well, right now, if I don't misremember that map that your uncle gave me,' answered Lofty, 'right now, we're comin' to a road called High Downs Road . . .'

At that moment Fanty gave a huge leap into the air.

'. . . guess we akshally *come* into High Downs Road,' said Lofty, '*and* crossed it. And right now Fanty is lepping over the hedge. What he'll do next is to take us up to Gallows Peak on the top of this here hill. Then he'll race off downhill through the Mist Curtain, and I reckon in five minutes from then we'll be havin' our cawfee and eatin' our chow in my pardner's cabin down on the range.'

But David was getting rather cross. To ride barefoot on a wild night, with nothing on but pyjamas and a dressing-gown, isn't the best way of keeping warm and comfortable. It was all right for Toby, because he had been sandwiched between Lofty and David and had been protected from the wind.

'Troll Woods go on for miles and miles,' David grumbled, 'and I bet we won't get out of them for *hours*. My feet are *frozen* . . .'

Already Fanty was plunging down the other side of Gallows Peak towards the dense forest but, as David spoke, Lofty halted the horse with a great cry of: 'Whoa, boy, whoa!'

'Did you say them woods was called Troll Woods, pardner?' he said, sharply. There was something in his voice that made David forget his cold feet, at least for the moment.

'Yes,' he answered.

'And hev you ever heard of any places in these woods called Groaning Cavern or Werewolf's Leap?' asked

Lofty, turning round to him and speaking very softly.

'Everybody knows them,' said David snappishly (he was sure he was going to have chilblains on his toes). 'They're just an old cave and a place where the river runs through a deep channel in the rocks.'

'Maybe, pardner, maybe,' answered Lofty, very patiently, 'but that proves ter me that these are the very Troll Woods I been warned about. We may soon be in great danger, pardner. I got to think a whiles, try to remember all I been taught about dealing with Trolls. Meantime, I see you're kinda freezefootulated. Jes' let me stoke up my pipe and we'll soon put that to rights. Pardner Toby, are you freezefootulated, too?'

'Treacle pudding,' mumbled Toby.

'Jumping catfish! I don't know what to do about *thet* complaint,' said Lofty.

'What complaint?' David asked. He was irritable . . . he felt sure now that all his toes had turned blue.

'Waal,' said Lofty, 'hevin' cold feet makes you freeze-footulated, so it stands to sense havin' treacle puddin' makes Toby treaclepudulated. And thet's a sickness I don't know nawthin' about, pardner.'

'But it's *not* an illness,' said David. 'Treacle pudding is something to eat and Toby likes it. He *dreams* about it. He even *talks* about it in his sleep. All night long, sometimes.'

'More treacle,' said Toby cosily. 'Um-yum!' And then he gave a loud snore.

'So thet's all it is!' said Lofty. 'He sure had me worried, pardner. Anyways, if he's able to sleep, then he ain't got cold feet. Nobody kin sleep with cold feet. So now, Fanty,' he said, slapping the horse's neck, 'let's see what we kin do about pardner David and his trouble.' And he began to puff and puff on his little clay pipe until the bowl glowed red and first sparks and then flames came roaring out of it so that soon his nose was glowing like a red-hot poker. 'If you'll jes' loosen yore hold on my belt, David,' he said, 'I guess we're about ready for you pardner.'

At that moment, out of the darkness below them,

there came something long and hard, yet rubbery, like a great hosepipe. It wrapped itself round David's waist and the next moment he felt himself whisked off the saddle and held up in the air with his feet in the great waves of heat that came from Lofty's pipe.

'Ain't nawthin' ter be feared of, pardner,' chuckled Lofty. 'Jes' relax an' toast your toes.'

Mind you, David *had* been on the point of crying out 'Help!' when he was whisked up into the air, but the moment he felt the lovely heat from Lofty's pipe around his feet he gave a great sigh of comfort.

'Lofty,' he said sleepily, 'I hope it doesn't make you tired, holding me up here like this.' He was feeling sorry now for having been so grumpy.

'Don't make *me* tired, pardner,' said Lofty, 'bekase t'ain't me thet's holding you up. It's Fanty.'

'Fanty!' David gasped. 'But how can a horse do that?'

'Thought I done told you about Fanty,' Lofty drawled, 'but I remember me now. Right back under your bedroom window I was jest 'bout to tell you when somebody axed me a question and it went right outa my mind. Didn't you never wonder why I call him "Fanty"? Waal, it's bekase he's part hoss and part elephant. He's an elephoss, pardner—he's got a hoss's body but he's got an elephant's trunk an' elephant's memory too. And it's his trunk, pardner David, thet's holdin' you up there to toast your toes. Guess you kin put him down now, Fanty, he's jes' about done to a turn.'

David found himself being gently lowered into his seat as Fanty set off again into the woods. 'Tuck your feet under the saddle,' advised Lofty, 'an' hold on tight to my belt each side of Toby so he don't fall off in his sleep. You were right, David,' Lofty added, 'in a manner of speakin'. If the Trolls were out in Troll Woods, it could take us hours to pick our way through the forest, from one hidin' place to another, trying to avoid them . . . and if we didn't manage to dodge 'em, pardner, we should never get out alive. Bekase the Trolls is death to travellers, pardner—didn't nobody never tell you that?'

'I don't really know anything about Trolls,' David said. 'I thought they were just things in fairy-tales.'

'I wish they was,' said Lofty, 'an' I hopes you'll never see a Troll *outside* a story book. Bekase Trolls is evil, pardner. Deadly, pardner. Trolls is killers.'

'Do you think we shall get through all right?' asked David, for Lofty's words gave him cold shivers.

'This time we got no need to worry,' said Lofty, to David's great relief. 'I been callin' to mind all thet your Uncle Cobwebb told me about Trolls and how to avoid meetin' 'em. This time o' year Trolls don't come out o' their holes in the ground and the rocks and the trees before eleven at night and it's now only just after ten. So we have a good hour o' safe travel in the woods and Fanty can do the rest o' the journey in 'bout five minutes, like I said. Giddy-up, Fanty, what you stoppin' fer?'

Fanty, however, didn't move.

'What's the matter?' asked David.

'Quiet,' said Lofty, 'he's pricking up his ears. Musta heard sump'n. He kin hear things afore we do.'

David and Lofty strained their ears in the darkness. Then, all at once, the air felt colder—not icy, but chill and clammy. Little eddies of wind rustled the underbrush and the dead leaves on the forest floor. And then, suddenly, they heard it: a slithering and a soft low hissing as though a thousand snakes were writhing all around them, near . . . and nearer . . . and nearer.

'What is it? What sh-shall we d-do, Lofty?' whispered David, his teeth chattering.

And Lofty answered, 'We cain't do anything now, pardner, 'cept stay right here where we are. We been ambushed, pardner. *The Trolls are all around us.*'

CHAPTER 4

SENTENCED BY THE TROLLS

AND so they stood, and waited fearfully for whatever was to happen. Meanwhile the hissing and whispering sounds grew ever closer. They seemed to come from the ground and from the trees and they were all around. And now David could begin to make out words among the hissing . . .

'Are all the netss ssslung ssafely, Trollknightss?'

'Yesss, Trollking. Sssafely fasstened. All sssecure.'

'You are cccertain there iss no way of esscape for these invaderss?'

'Cccertain, Trollking.'

'Then sstand to armss, Trollsssoldiers, and uncover your lampss.'

And, in a flash the forest was lit with millions of tiny lights. David and Lofty—for Toby was still sound asleep—saw that they were completely surrounded. The lamps glowed everywhere: upon the forest floor, on the bushes, around the tree trunks and along all the branches, from the lowest to the topmost. Gleaming silken nets, hanging from the trees, enclosed them on all sides and were even pegged across the ground so that no horse, not even a horse like Fanty, could have attempted to gallop off without unseating his riders.

And now, David and Lofty looked for the first time upon the dreaded Trolls!

WARNING

The next few sentences will tell you what David and Lofty saw, that is, exactly what Trolls are *like*, but if you don't want to read about these horrible creatures, just leave that bit out and go straight on to the place marked like this ⊠ on the next page. In that case it would be best not to look at the drawing of the Trolls on page 22 either, although it's quite true that no *drawing* of a Troll could be as horrible as a Troll really *is*.

A Troll, even by itself, is an ugly sight. Try to imagine an egg, standing with the narrow end up. Then make that egg as big as a football. Except for a little tiny bit at the top, where there are two evil red eyes, glowing like coals and without any eyelashes, the whole creature is surrounded by a dense mass of bushy black hair. The Troll stands on two scaly claws—no one has ever seen a Troll's legs—and these claws stick out from under the great blanket of hair for about twelve inches. The Troll does not walk with these claws. It does not hop. It just sort of sidles along the ground, sometimes at incredible speed, making a nasty, soft, slithering sound. It hasn't any hands, but at the end of its short and bony arms are a thick thumb and a skinny fore-finger, each with a long, curved and very sharp nail. They look just like a lobster's pincers and when a Troll is angry he snaps them together until they rattle like castanets.

This is what happened now as the Trolls, in their thousands, hissed and sidled about the forest floor. Every tree branch was black with them, stretching and flexing their long, scaly feet like vultures and sometimes hanging upside down like bats and reaching out their giant pincers towards their victims.

[×] Lofty whispered, 'Say, pardner, who d'you think's the boss o' this outfit?'

'Look down to your left,' said David softly. 'There's a bunch of Trolls with helmets with horns on each side. They must be the Trollknights. And there's one in the middle with a kind of a crown . . . see?'

'I see him,' said Lofty. 'Now watch me knock that crown into the middle o' next week.' And, like light-ning, both his hands flashed to his pistols.

But the Trolls were quicker. At his first move, two of them swung head down from an overhanging branch. Their great pincers snatched the pistols from Lofty's hands and hurled them into the blackness of the undergrowth. A vast angry clacking of claws broke out all around, but faded to silence as a great hiss came from the Trollknights.

Just three among the thousands of evil Trolls who am-bushed Lofty and David and Toby in Troll Woods. The Trollking is the biggest and the others are the Troll-astronomer and the Trollchef. Trolls sort of hiss when they talk, and the most terrible thing that can happen to a Troll-child is to develop a lisp.

'Sssilence! The Trollking ssspeakss!'

'Ssstrangers,' hissed the Trollking, 'why do you tresspass on our landsss?'

'We ain't trespassing,' replied Lofty, 'bekase this ain't your territory, except between eleven o'clock at night and dawn. As well you know, you 'airy old 'orror.'

'As well I know,' hissed the Trollking. 'Trollass-stronomer, pleasse tell thiss persson what the time iss.'

'Your Majessty,' answered a very fat Troll. 'It iss now precisssely eleven hours p.m. plusss twenty minutes plusss sixxx and three-tenthsss sssecondsss.'

'Sso, you sssee, you *are* trespassing,' said the Trollking to Lofty. 'It *iss* after eleven p.m. and sso thiss *iss* our territory.'

Lofty spluttered with anger. He dived a hand into his waistcoat pocket and pulled out a huge silver watch on a great chain.

'And this watch here,' he shouted, 'which is a gen-u-wine fifteen lever, twenty-jewel three-dollar crownometer, says that that's all nonsense. T'ain't eleven twenty anything—it's *ten* twenty. You-all oughta be in bed fer another forty minutes.'

The Trollking did not answer at once. He seemed to be shaking like a great black jelly.

'Lofty,' whispered David, 'I think he's laughing at you. Are you sure you're right about the time?'

'This watch never let me down yet,' said Lofty. 'But I 'gree the old buzzard is certainly laughing—and I don't like it.'

But the Trollking was speaking again.

'Oh sssilly, sssilly, sssilly persssson!' he hissed. 'Sssurely you know that Trolltime is one hour ahead of earthland time? When you were about to enter Troll Woods you ssshould have put your watch forward one hour. But you forgot, didn't you, sssilly persssson?'

There was no need for Lofty to reply. The look of dismay on his face showed how right the Trollking was. The whole seething mass of Trolls hissed and fizzled with evil merriment. They jiggled about, they kicked their scaly toes in the air and those on the trees jumped up and down until the branches beneath them cracked and threatened to break.

'Pardner David,' said Lofty, 'I sure am sorry . . .'

'It could have happened to anybody, Lofty,' said David. 'And whatever happens, we're going to see this thing through together. I'm sure Toby would say the same thing.'

And now, when the Trolls were practically out of breath from laughing, the Trollking stepped forward.

'Trollsss all,' he hissed, 'it hasss been proved that thesse persssonsss are tressspasssersss on our landsss. What shall be the sssentencce?'

And from the urging mass of evil blackness there came the one word: *'Death!'*

CHAPTER 5

TREACLE PUDDING OR YOUR LIVES!

WHEN this hissing and sizzling of the Trolls had died down a little, the Trollking addressed Lofty and the boys.

'Well, ssstrangersss,' he said, 'you have heard the verdict. But we Trollsss are really very kind people . . .'

'Sez you!' muttered Lofty.

'. . . and we alwaysss,' said the Trollking, 'give the convicted persssonsss a chanccce to essscape the death sssentencce. I am going to asssk you a question and if any of you anssswersss it correctly we shall ssset you all free. The question isss thisss: *do you know anything that Trollsss don't know*? Think well before you ansswer. Dissscusss it among yourssselvesss if you like. We are in no hurry.'

'I don't trust him,' David whispered to Lofty.

'I think they're simply playing with us,' answered Lofty.

Toby just gave a loud snore.

'I say, Lofty,' said David, 'if we've all got to answer the question that means we'll have to wake Toby and he hasn't seen a Troll yet. I hope he won't be frightened...'

And then David nearly fell off the elephorse with surprise as Toby whispered fiercely, 'I'm not frightened at all. I've been awake for the last twenty minutes. And I've got an idea...'

'Well, tell us, Toby,' said Lofty, 'fer your pardner Lofty's brain is sure parammalised at this moment.'

'Listen,' whispered Toby. 'Whatever I say or do let them think I'm doing it in my sleep. Don't pretend to wake me unless they ask you to.'

'But what *are* you going to do?' asked David.

'Wait and see,' said Toby, and it was no use David trying to argue for at that moment the Trollking spoke.

'Time isss up. Now you, perssson in the big hat, what do you know that Trollsss don't know?'

'Waal,' answered Lofty. 'I kin lassoo a steer and I bet thet's sump'n you ain't never done nor will do, you moth-eaten old floor mop!'

The Trollking thought this over. Then he said, 'We don't use lassoosss and there are no steersss in Troll Woodsss. But if any Troll *had* a lassssoo and he found a ssssteer, then he *could* lasssoo it. Ssso you're wrong. Only two chanccces left to sssave your livesss.'

The Trollking pointed his bony claw at David.

'Now it'sss your turn,' he said.

'I know the longest word in the world,' said David promptly. 'It's supercalifragilisticexpialidocious.'

The Trollking looked startled.

'*Not* the longessst word,' smirked the Trollastronomer, stepping forward. 'I know one jussst asss long. It'sss polifrasticontinomimegalondulation. It'sss the sssame length—thirty-four lettersss.'

'There'sss your sssecond chanccce gone,' hissed the Trollking, and all the Trolls jiggled and fizzled with evil glee. But right at that very moment, Toby gave a great snore and said, in a sleepy, dreamy kind of voice, 'Oh,
25

yum-yum! Wonderful, wonderful! My very own Treacle Trollpudding!'

A great quiver of interest swept through the Trolls as they heard the words. Then Toby snored again and he began to sing sleepily:

> *In all the wide world*
> *There's nothing so good in*
> *The recipe-books*
> *As my Treacle Trollpudding:*
> > *My Treacle Trollpudding,*
> > *My Treacle Trollpudding,*
> > *My very own, patented, Treacle Trollpudding.*

Then Toby gave another long snore and seemed to be sound asleep again.

'What isss thisss?' exclaimed the Trollking. 'Trollchef! Why have you never made us a Treacle Trollpudding?'

And in a despairing whisper, that sounded like a tiny kettle going off the boil, the Trollchef answered, 'Because I d-d-don't know how to, M-Majesty.'

'Throw him into hisss own cooking-pot,' hissed the Trollking, and the poor Trollchef was hustled away. A great clamour arose from the Trolls: 'Wake the ssstranger! Make him tell usss the recipe!'

But, as Toby gave another snore and began his song again, the Trollking raised his hand.

'Sssilence!' he commanded. 'He may tell usss in his sssleep what he might refussse to tell usss if he wasss awake. Lisssten ...'

And Toby went on with his sleepy song ...

> *It makes Trollhair shiny*
> *And silky and sleek,*
> *It makes Trollclaws stronger*
> *To tear and to tweak:*
> > *My Treacle Trollpudding,*
> > *My Treacle Trollpudding,*
> > *My very own, patented, Treacle Trollpudding.*

It makes Trollminds keener,
It makes Trolleyes shine,
But the recipe's secret—
And the secret is mine ...
   My Treacle Trollpudding,
   My Treacle Trollpudding,
   My very own, patented, Treacle Trollpudding.

The Trolls wer now sizzling with curiosity and impatience.

Toby gave another great yawn, and then he made some stretchy waking-up noises and at last he said sleepily, 'Where are we, David? What's happened? Who are these people?'

'Welcome to the land of the Trollsss,' said the Trollking in an oily sort of voice. 'Young perssson, I have graciously decccided that you shall be allowed to make usss a disssh of your famous Treacle Trollpudding.'

'But that's my secret recipe!' exclaimed Toby, as if he were very surprised and alarmed. 'Who told you about it?'

'If you want to keep sssecretsss,' hissed the Trollking playfully, 'then you shouldn't talk in your sssleep.'

'But I bet I didn't tell you the recipe in my sleep,' said Toby.

'You didn't,' said the Trollking, 'and that's why you are going to show usss how to make the pudding.'

'No, I'm not!' said Toby firmly.

'Then we shall kill you,' hissed the Trollking, in a sizzling temper.

'If you kill me, then you'll *never* know the recipe!' answered Toby promptly.

The Trollking fought down his temper and then he said craftily, 'Very well. If you show usss how to make the Treacle Trollpudding, I will graciously ssspare the livesss of both you and your friendsss. It will be your fault if we have to kill them because you refusse. Why not ssspeak to them and asssk them what they would like you to do? We will wait while you dissscusss it!'

27

'Lofty, David,' whispered Toby. 'My plan's beginning to work. Will you trust me to carry it out?'

'Pardner,' said Lofty, 'if you got a plan to get us out of here and away from these walking floor-mops, then I'm with you. You go right ahead and I'll do anything you want me to.'

'But, *Toby*!' exclaimed David. 'You've never made a pudding, *any* sort of pudding! Even if there is such a thing as a Treacle Trollpudding, I bet you haven't the faintest idea what goes into it.'

And do you know what Toby did? He actually giggled.

'I haven't,' he admitted. 'But then, remember, *neither have the trolls*.'

And before either David or Lofty could make any comment he raised his right arm and called in a loud voice. 'Trollking! In exchange for our lives, I will make you the biggest and best Treacle Trollpudding that the world has ever seen!'

CHAPTER 6

THE DOOM OF THE TROLLS

THE Trolls hopped and hissed for joy. Quickly the nets on the ground were dismantled and, on the Trollking's order, Fanty was led through the forest towards a great wall of rock in which gaped the black mouth of a vast cavern.

When they reached the entrance, the Trolls kept Toby with them while Fanty, David and Lofty were taken up a little hill, on one side of the cave. Here Fanty was tethered and Lofty and David, each trussed like mummies in saddle blankets, were bound to a tree.

Meanwhile, below, the Trolls had thronged into the enormous cavern, thousands of them hanging like huge clusters of black bats, upside-down from the festoons of stalactites in the roof, holding their tiny Troll lamps to light up the scene below where masses of eager Trolls clustered around a vast iron cooking-pot. In a cleared space before it stood the Trollking and Toby, flanked by the bodyguard of Trollknights. Near them the Troll-chef—who had been nearly half-boiled when the Troll-king changed his mind about the sentence of death—sat dripping on a boulder.

'He will make a note of all the ingredientsss asss you order them,' said the Trollking to Toby. 'Now prepare the Treacle Trollpudding.'

'First of all,' said Toby, 'I want to know if you have any flour, salt, baking powder, eggs, powdered ginger, sugar, yeast, milk and of course, treacle—lots of treacle.'

'All that and more,' replied the Trollking, proudly. 'Every farm, every housse and every ssshop for milesss around paysss tribute to the Trollsss. Give your ordersss.'

And Toby did . . and as he spoke, Trolls rushed off down this corridor or that to bring the materials from the Trolls' storerooms deep underground.

Outside, up on the hill, David and Lofty listened, amazed and puzzled.

'Forty sacks of flour!' repeated David. 'Ten gallons of milk . . . fifteen pounds of yeast . . . fifteen bags of sugar . . . eighty tins of baking powder . . . sixty barrels of treacle. Whatever does Toby think he's doing, Lofty?'

'We must believe he *knows* what he's doing, pardner,' answered Lofty, 'bekase Toby thinks he can get us out of here. But if thet conjorumallation of stuff is a puddin' I'm durn glad the Trolls are going ter eat it and not me!'

Meanwhile, in the cavern, the eager Trolls were running up and down long ladders set against the cooking-pot and emptying the strange mixture of ingredients into it.

At last Toby said, 'The Treacle Trollpudding is ready for cooking, Trollking. Light the fire under the pot and seal the iron lid with wet clay to keep in the wonderful flavour. Cook over a fierce blaze for twenty minutes and it will be ready.'

All the Trolls began to lick their lips, making a horrible, slithery, slurpy sound. The Trollking called, 'Trollchef, have you got everything down in your recccipe book?'

'Yesss, Your Majesty,' was the answer.

'Count the minutesss, Trollassstronomer,' said the Trollking. The Trollastronomer stepped forward and pulled out a great iron watch.

'The firssst minute hasss already passsed,' he hissed.

'And now,' said the Trollking, in a sizzly kind of chuckle, 'sssince we no longer need the sservicccesss of thisss young perssson, take him outssside and tie him up with the othersss. After we have enjoyed our Treacle Trollpudding, we will ssslay them, all three.'

'But you said you'd set us all free if I told you the recipe!' protested Toby. And then the Trollking revealed the full depths of his treachery.

'Sssilly perssson,' he hissed—while the whole black mass of Trolls fizzled with glee—'once Trollsss have got what they want, they don't keep promisssesss. Take him away!'

A couple of Trollknights led Toby up the hillside, fastened him alongside the others, and then slithered swiftly down to the cavern again to join the hungry hissing crowd, eagerly watching the crackling fire that blazed beneath the huge cooking-pot.

It was a long, long time before anyone spoke. But at last Lofty said, 'I sure don't know what your plan was, pardner Toby, but seems it's kinda gone wrong. Still I guess you done your best, Toby, and thanks fer tryin'.'

'But it's *not* gone wrong!' replied Toby. 'It's going very well.'

'How can you say it's going well?' David objected, 'when they're going to kill us as soon as they've finished their meal?'

From below they heard the Trollastronomer call, 'Fifteen minutesss have elapsssed, Trollking.'

'David,' said Toby, 'tell me something. When Mother makes bread why does she use yeast, or sometimes baking powder?'

'Because when they're mixed with the other stuff and warmed, they make gas and that makes the dough rise, and . . .'

'Well, then,' said Toby with a giggle, 'there's going to be a lot of gas in that treacle pudding, because it's got fifteen pounds of yeast *and* eighty tins of baking powder in it. And the gas can't get out because the lid is sealed down . . .'

'Toby!' exclaimed David. 'What a smashing idea!' He felt terribly proud of his younger brother.

'Smashing, pardners, is the right word,' chuckled Lofty. 'Them whistling, walking flue-brushes down there are settin' round a kinda homemade bomb, just awaitin' fer it to bust!'

From below they heard the Trollastronomer hiss, 'The sixxxteenth minute has elapsssed, Trollking. Only four minutesss remain before the . . .'

But he got no further. For at that moment, with a gigantic, ear-shattering roar, the huge cooking-pot exploded, hurling the Trolls in their thousands out through the opening of the cavern like a terrific shower of black snowballs. Behind them the rocks shattered and the roof of the cavern collapsed, sealing forever the Trolls from their home under the hill. And with this breaking of the Trolls' power, the great silken nets they had hung from the trees dissolved and faded away and the cords that bound Lofty and the boys snapped like burned thread.

Warmly wrapped in the saddle-blankets, David and Toby mounted behind Lofty, and Fanty turned along the track that led out of the wood. Around them, on trees and in the bushes beside the path, treacle-covered Trolls whimpered and wiggled their claws helplessly, unable to escape from the branches to which they were stuck. With their hair matted tightly round them, they looked like little burned-out match-sticks.

As Fanty cantered out from Troll Woods the sun rose behind a great bank of mist that faced them, making it into an enormous shining curtain.

'There 'tis, pardners!' cried Lofty. 'There's the Mist Curtain and once through that you'll be in Lofty's country.'

He put Fanty to a gallop. The elephorse stretched his trunk forward, sniffing the air. His hooves thundered on the rocky path as they shot towards the shining Mist Curtain at breakneck speed.

'Hold tight, pardners!' yelled Lofty.

Then, to his ear-splitting *Yippeee!*, Fanty soared from the ground, carrying Lofty, David and Toby into a cloud of blinding light.

CHAPTER 7

THE MESSAGE IN THE SMOKE

As they plunged on and on through the golden mist the air grew warm, then hot, then hotter still.

'Gettin' near my country, now, pardners,' said Lofty happily, and just at that moment they heard Fanty's hooves begin to clatter on hard ground, the cloud thinned, and they found themselves cantering among great yellow boulders up a steep, sandy hill while the sun blazed down on them from a cloudless, steely-blue sky. At the top of the hill Lofty brought the elephorse to a halt and they dismounted.

'Wall, here we are, pardners!' cried Lofty. 'Look down thar on a real man's country . . .'

Below them stretched a wide, bare plain, encircled by two curved ridges of almost bare rock—rock carved by the weather into fantastic and sometimes frightening shapes. There was not a tree to be seen anywhere, in fact the only tree-like living things were the scattered giant cacti that looked (as Toby said later) like railway signals that had grown spikes all over.

Both David and Toby were relieved to feel really warm after their night in Troll Woods, but there was a gnawing feeling inside them that told them it was time for breakfast and that bacon and eggs would be a much more attractive sight than all that rock and sand.

'It's very . . . very . . . er, *empty* scenery, Lofty, isn't it?' said Toby.

Lofty understood and laughed.

'Guess you'd like it better, pardners, ef you hed your feet under a table and eatin' irons in your hands,' he said. 'Ef you look down thar you'll see a glimpse of water. Thet's Gopher Creek and right alongside it you'll see a cabin. Wal, in thet cabin is Lefty and he's waitin' right now fer my signal ter bile the cawfee an' put on the frying pan. Jes lissen ter me let out a whoop thet'll bring him jumpin' through the door.' And Lofty drew in a huge breath, threw back his head and cupped his hands round his mouth.

But the whoop never came. For at that moment Fanty curled his trunk round his master's neck, lifted him from the ground and planted him down again facing one of the great rock peaks across the valley. Lofty let out his breath in a long, low whistle and pointed to the distant ridge.

'See thet, pardners?' he said. 'Know what it is?'

'It's smoke,' said Toby.

'A volcano,' suggested David, as spurt after spurt of smoke rose into the still air.

'It's no volcano,' answered Lofty, 'but it's something just as dangerous. That's an Injun smoke-signal. They're on the warpath, pardners, and they're callin' all the tribe together fer an attack.'

'But who are they going to attack?' asked David.

'Thet's what I'm gonna find out,' said Lofty, grimly, digging into his waistcoat pocket for his stubby little pipe and lighting it. 'Come along, Fanty, you've got more wind than I hev—jes' puff some smoke out o' this while I send a message.' And he pushed the pipe into the end of Fanty's trunk.

The elephorse certainly had good stout lungs, for in a few seconds he was puffing out a steady stream of blue smoke which Lofty kept interrupting by using his wide cowboy hat. On the distant mountain the smoke signals stopped for a few minutes until Lofty had finished his message.

'Thanks, Fanty,' he said, as he stuffed his pipe back in his pocket. 'You done used up all my terbakker on that message but I guess I shan't hev to send another.'

'What did you ask them?' said Toby. 'And how did you learn Indian smoke-signal language?'

'Larned it from my good friends the Moccasin tribe,' grinned Lofty. 'Don't you go a-thinking that *we're* at war with the Injuns—not on the Double C Ranch we ain't: they're friends—and very good friends they are, too . . .' But just at that moment David cried, 'Look! They're signalling back.'

Lofty shaded his eyes with his hand as he concentrated on reading the message in the smoke. Suddenly he cried, 'Sufferin' catfish!' Then, 'What's this?' And then, a moment later, 'The double-crossin' galoots . . . !'

'What is it? What do they say? What's wrong?' said David and Toby as the smoke signals suddenly ceased.

'It's the Moccasin tribe . . . our *friends*, the Moccasins,' answered Lofty, bitterly. 'They've broken the pipe of peace, the tomahawks are out and the scalping knives are sharpened. They're on the warpath against the Double C Ranch and the first place they're a-ridin' for ter burn and kill is Lefty's cabin just down thar. I don't know what's behind all this but there's only one thing to do—I got to try to stop 'em.'

'Not by yourself,' said David stoutly. 'We're going to help.'

'Sure we are,' Toby said. 'Couldn't we lay an ambush for them?'

'Without a single gun between us, pardners?' replied Lofty. 'Remember, the Trolls threw my shootin' irons away.'

'Well, let's get down to the cabin and warn your friend at least,' said David.

'He'll hev guns enough fer him and me, I guess,' said Lofty, 'but not enough fer you, pardners, sure-lee. My idea is this: the Injuns ain't expectin' to find two men in the cabin, an' I reckon the raidin' party won't be in great strength, so I guess me and Lefty hev a chance of keepin' 'em off for some time. Now, as soon as the shootin' begins, they'll be too busy with us to be lookin' over their shoulders, so thet's the time when you, David, and you, Tony, lead Fanty down to the plain. Keep under cover behind the rocks. Then, soon as you're on the level, leap on his back, hit the trail for the Double C Ranch and get reinforcements. Fanty knows the way home, don't worry.'

David and Toby didn't like leaving Lofty, but it really did seem the better plan, so Lofty left them and began to make his way down the hillside. They watched him clamber down and saw his tiny figure run across the plain to the cabin. Then they heard his ear-piercing whistle and saw a long, lanky figure run out of the cabin almost dancing with joy, waving a great frying pan and banging on it with a huge soup ladle in welcome.

And at that moment, yelling and screaming, war plumes flying and tomahawks gleaming, a murderous throng of Moccasin braves thundered from the mouth of the valley upon the two unarmed cowboys.

CHAPTER 8

FANTY SAVES THE DAY

Down below, Lofty and Lefty turned and dashed for the shelter of the cabin as the screaming mob bore down on them. Lefty held the frying pan like a shield and it was lucky he had it for several arrows bounced from it with a clang before the two cowboys leaped through the heavy wooden door and slammed it behind them.

The Indians now set their horses to circle the shack, shooting off their arrows from all sides, and David and Toby started to work their way with Fanty down the hillside, keeping as far as they could in the shelter of large rocks and boulders. At length they reached the level ground and rested behind a huge boulder while they prepared for the dash across the plain, where there was nothing to hide them from the enemy. Beside the boulder a huge tree-cactus—the kind that Toby had said reminded him of a crazy railway signal—lay on the ground.

'The boulder must have rolled right down this hillside to uproot that great thing,' said David. 'I hope there are no more loose ones to do the same to us!'

But he forgot the danger when Toby said suddenly, 'Look at those two Indians over there. What are they doing?'

To one side of the shack and screened from the view of Lofty and his friend by the circling warriors, two young braves had lit a fire and were now unloading something from the back of a tethered horse. Whatever it was, they appeared to be dividing it into small piles and tying each to the head of an arrow. As the boys watched, an Indian galloped out from the band encircling the shack. As he swept past them, the men at the fire plunged an arrow into the flames and held it up to him, a great ball of fire flaming round the tip.

'They're fire-arrows!' cried David. 'The Indians are going to burn the shack down with Lofty and his friend inside.'

And he was right. For now brave after brave was passing the fire, seizing a blazing brand and galloping again round the shack, shooting his burning arrow high into the air so that it should drop on the roof.

'What's the use of going for reinforcements now?' cried Toby. 'They'll probably be burned to death before we can even reach the ranch.'

'We ought to attack the Indians,' said David.

A deep, angry rumbling sound came from Fanty's trunk and he pawed the ground and showed the whites of his eyes.

'Fanty thinks so, too,' answered Toby, 'and so do I— but we've no guns—nothing. If only we'd *some* kind of weapon . . . something at least to—to—*hit* them with.'

36

And that was what gave David an idea. He stooped and seized the broken trunk of the fallen tree-cactus. 'Come and help me, Toby,' he said.

Toby joined him and they heaved together. 'We can't lift this, even between us,' Toby said, panting.

'I know,' answered David, 'but I want Fanty to see what we're trying to do and to realise that we can't manage it by ourselves.'

Even as he spoke Fanty's trunk pushed them gently aside, curled itself round the stem and, as easily as if it had been a feather, lifted the huge cactus up high.

'Good old Fanty!' cried David. He clambered into the saddle and pulled Toby up behind him. 'Hold on to me tight, pardner,' he said, gripping the reins. 'Now, Fanty, remember: Giddup! Lofty's in danger. We've got to save him from the Indians . . .' And, with a great throaty bellow of rage, Fanty shot forward like a cannonball towards the yelling mob of warriors.

The Indians were so intent on their murderous scheme that the attackers were within a few yards of them before the alarm was given. First to see the approaching vengeance was the Moccasins' medicine man. He hauled on his reins in terror, throwing all those behind him into confusion as he screamed and urged his horse into flight. But it was too late for him, or for any of the Indian raiders, for fifteen feet of spiky cactus rose and fell, rose and fell among them putting panic into horse and rider and scattering them far and wide. With David and Toby screeching their own war-cry the elephorse pursued the fleeing Indians, herding them together and driving them in terror to their homeward trail through the valley.

Only when there was no longer a Moccasin in sight did Fanty toss away the cactus and canter back to the cabin where Lofty and Lefty, having knocked the burning arrows from the roof before they could do any harm, were waiting to greet them.

The tall cowboy, who had had to bend almost double to get through the door, introduced himself in a brief speech that was like music in their ears.

37

'Greetings, new pardners,' he said. 'You needs food—there's bacon and egg jest gone into the pan. You needs drink—there's cawfee coming to the bile. You needs wash—there's water, soap and towels. You needs proper cowboys clothes fer these parts—there's two suits ready I got from the store soon's I hed your measurements from the Chief. Come right in and make yourselves at home!'

That night, while Fanty stood in his stall at one end of the shack contentedly munching away, the boys and their friends sat round the stove and talked.

Lofty and Lefty were completely baffled about the Indian attack. 'The Chief—thet's your Uncle Cobwebb,' said Lofty, 'smoked the pipe of peace with Chief Bald Eagle years ago and we been friends with the Moccasins ever since. Some folks say Injuns are treacherous, but we never found 'em so—leastways not until this business. The Moccasins never rustled our cattle. We always respected their territory. Now they come on the warpath to scalp and burn. Why?'

'You're right,' agreed Lefty. 'It's not like the Moccasins to turn on their friends. What we've got to find out is what made 'em do it. But right now I say we git to bed.'

He smiled at Lofty and they both looked at David and Toby, whose heads were beginning to nod. 'I guess we all had enough excitement for one day, pardners,' he said.

And then, suddenly, in a whisper that brought them wide awake and tense, Lefty said, 'Don't move, don't speak anyone. Sump'n's movin' on the roof!'

CHAPTER 9

WHO ARE THE KILLERS?

THEY all fell silent, but whatever kind of noise it was that Lefty had heard, it was not repeated. Lofty moved, soft-footed, to one side of the window. Then, with a

38

broad wink to the others, he yawned very loudly and said, 'Jes' open the window, pardner, ter give us a bit more air, an' let's git to our bunks. Good night.' And he turned down the oil-lamp to a glimmer and opened the window. Outside the sand and the rocks reflected the pale light of the moon.

For a full minute—and if you want to know just how long one minute can be, try counting up to sixty very slowly—for a full minute there was utter silence. Then they heard a very light, scrapey, scratchy sound from the roof.

Then, silhouetted against the moonlight, they saw two legs slowly descending until the feet were resting on the window-sill. Then, as if the mysterious intruder was still holding on to the edge of the roof, the legs were followed by a slim body until the person was sitting on the window ledge with his legs inside. Then the head and arms came into view . . . and then . . .

Then came a sudden sharp scream of mingled rage and fear, the light was turned up and there, firmly gripped in a coil of Fanty's trunk, kicked and struggled a young Indian brave, bare to the waist and covered in war-paint.

In a flash Lefty had knocked the gleaming knife from the youth's grasp and pulled his arms behind his back, while Lofty dived to the floor and seized the intruder's ankles in his powerful grip.

'And now, if you'll jes' reach me that lariat off'n the hook there,' remarked Lefty calmly, 'we'll string up this young turkey-cock so's he cain't do any harm.' In a matter of seconds the intruder was trussed beyond all possibility of escape and Fanty withdrew his trunk—but not before giving the Indian's ear a sharp tweak that made him quiver with helpless rage.

But now Lofty had planted himself, feet apart and hands on hips, in front of the captive and was staring up at him and puffing his pipe reflectively. David and Toby could hardly keep back a smile at the sight of the burly little cowboy tilting his head far back in order to look into the eyes of the Indian boy. 'For that's all he

39

really is,' murmured Toby to his brother. 'He can't be a lot older than you.'

At the side of the Indian, Lefty, long and lanky, was lounging with his elbows spread out on the rafters of the cabin and his head almost touching the ridge of the roof—but although he was smiling lazily, his keen grey eyes were alert as he gazed down on his cowboy friend and the Moccasin.

Lofty continued to suck on his pipe without saying anything but he did not move his eyes from those of the Indian, who gazed back at him with hatred. After what seemed an hour, Lofty reached up a long arm and tapped the other on the chest. 'Speak!' he demanded.

'No,' answered the other. 'You kill me—but I no speak.'

'I say Moccasin tribe are cowards,' said Lofty deliberately.

There was no reply, but the prisoner's eyes flashed murderously.

'If Moccasins steal into other man's wigwam when he sleeps, then Moccasins fear to fight by daylight. So Moccasins are cowards.'

Still the other did not answer. Lofty reached out and lifted the Indian's knife from the floor, and held it up before his face.

'Moccasins, I say, *are* cowards!' he taunted. 'Moccasins send boy to kill for them because they afraid.' This was too much for the prisoner.

'Old beetle, you lie!' he cried.

But Lofty went on. 'Moccasins send hundred warriors here this day to kill one man—' and he pointed to Lefty—'so I say Moccasins are cowards.'

'Lie . . . lie!'

But Lofty would not stop. 'And I say worse!' he thundered. 'Moccasins speak lies. Chief Bald Eagle smokes pipe of peace with Chief Double C Ranch. Now he makes war on friends . . .'

But by now the prisoner had reached breaking point. Struggling with his bonds, he cried, *'No, no! Chief Cobwebb broke pipe of peace. Double C cowboys raid our camps by night. Kill people, horses. Ride away . . .'*

He stopped, panting, his eyes fixed on the face of Lofty, whose mouth had fallen open, whose pipe had dropped to the floor unnoticed and who was standing as if turned to stone.

It was the voice of Lefty, leaning over the rafters above, that broke the silence.

'I know you,' he said to the Indian. 'You are Little Cloud, son of Chief Bald Eagle and a brave warrior. Hear me: Chief Cobwebb is still the friend of the Moccasins.'

But the Indian interrupted.

'I see truth in his eyes,' he said, nodding towards Lofty. 'But after attacks we find cowboy shirt with Double C mark and one right boot and spur with same Cobwebb brand.'

Then Lofty spoke—and he spoke not to Little Cloud but to David and Toby. 'Do you believe your Uncle Cobwebb would 'llow things like this ter be done?' he asked, and as they cried 'No!' he went on, 'Then there's only one way to stop the fightin' while we get the news to the Chief and he starts a-lookin' into this murderous business. Are you willin' ter help, pardners? Yes? . . . Well, then, hear me, Chief Little Cloud. These boys are strangers just come from across the Great Water. They are of the blood of Chief Cobwebb. They say they will come with you and be hostages of Moccasins . . . until we find truth.'

Lofty reached out and slashed the bonds that bound the young warrior. 'Now,' he added, 'you free to say "yes", free to say "no", and free to go return to your tribe. What say?'

The Indian rubbed his chafed wrists and pondered. Then he looked gravely at David and Toby.

At length he said, 'It is good. They come.'

'Then git some sleep,' said Lofty, 'and eat and leave at dawn.' Then he asked, 'Does Little Cloud need this?' And he handed back to the Indian the long keen knife that they had taken from him.

Little Cloud took the weapon and looked at it a

moment. Then, stooping, he put the blade beneath his foot and, with a quick movement, snapped it in two and flung the pieces through the window.

Lifting a hand, he said, 'Peace!' And then he lay down on the floor and slept.

CHAPTER 10

THE MENACE OF THE UGUDUGU-DJUK

THE thing that David and Toby were most looking forward to next morning, when they put on their new cowboy clothes, was wearing a broad leather belt, weighted down by a holster and six-shooter on each hip. They were disappointed, however, for Lofty refused to let them carry arms—not even a knife.

'You see, pardners,' he said, 'you got ter show the Injuns that you put yourselves entirely at their mercy. Thet proves how much you believe thet your Uncle Septimus Cobwebb is really their friend. You'll need to be pretty brave, pardners, fer I know they won't exakly welcome you . . . they ain't all as reasonable as Little Cloud . . . and they may jes' get the idea you been sent as spies and try to make you confess.'

'How would they do that?' asked David, and both boys began to feel cold shivers go down their spines.

'Wal, the usual way,' said Lofty, 'is ter tie you to a pole and light a circle of fire all round. Then they start a kind o' war-dance, rompin' round the fire and shootin' an arrow, or throwin' a tomahawk, now and then—not to hit you, but just to miss by about an inch so thet you think the next one is going to kill you fer sure. And they yell and scream and stop now and then to push the fire a bit nearer and bit nearer to the pole till your pants begin to smoulder and you think it sure is the end. If you kin go as fur as thet without breakin' down, then they reckon you must be speakin' true and they put out the fire and cut you down. And from then on they're pretty friendly.'

'Do you think that's likely to happen to us, Lofty?' asked Toby.

'I don't say it will, pardner, but mebbe . . . jes' mebbe. Question is: do you feel you're brave enough to stand it and still keep silent?'

'I don't know,' said David. 'Do you, Toby?' And as Toby shook his head, David went on, 'But if it *does* happen, we'll try our best to be brave.'

'And no cowboy could say better, pardners,' said Lofty heartily. 'Now, although you cain't carry a gun or a knife, there's one thing I *kin* give you. See this?' And he held out to David a thin little bamboo tube, about four inches long. 'This kin be used once only and then only if you think it's ab-so-*loot*-ly necessary. It's not a weapon. All it does is to call a messenger if you want to send something to your Uncle Septimus. Even if you're searched, nobody is goin' ter think this little piece o' wood is anythin' important. Now stick it in your pocket, quick, bekase here's Lefty and Little Cloud bringing in the water fer the cawfee.'

Nothing was said during the meal, but it was clear that the two cowboys and Little Cloud had been talking over the situation for at length Little Cloud rose and, lifting his hand, said, 'Wah! Hear me: it is agreed that the two little chiefs of Chief Cobwebb shall come to Moccasin tribe as pledge that Cobwebb cowboys remain friends of Moccasins and do not attack them.'

'It is so,' said Lofty.

'And you will tell this to Chief Cobwebb. And for space of one moon . . .' ('Thet means for 28 days, pardners,' whispered Lefty to the boys) '. . . for the space of one moon, Chief Cobwebb shall gather all his cowboys at the Double C Ranch . . .'

'It is so,' said Lofty.

'And if Moccasin tribe attacked during that time by cowboys . . .'

'They won't be from the Double C Ranch, Little Cloud,' said Lofty.

'. . . but if Moccasins can *prove* Double C cowboys among attackers, then . . .'

Lofty looked at David and Toby. 'You know what's comin' now, pardners, don't you?' he said, and David and Toby nodded.

'. . . then little Cobwebb Chiefs will be despatched to Happy Hunting Grounds,' finished Little Cloud.

'In plain English,' said Lefty, 'thet means the Moccasins will kill you.'

'So,' said Lofty, 'ef you got any feelin's thet your Uncle Septimus is likely to let you down and break his word to the Moccasins, now's your chance to say you won't go.'

David looked at Toby, and Toby looked back at David and nodded, and David said, 'We go with Little Cloud. We know Uncle Septimus wouldn't break his word, don't we, Toby?'

And Toby answered, 'Sure, pardner.'

Little Cloud rose. 'It is good,' he said. 'The Little Chiefs will follow me to Moccasin camp.'

'And Lefty an' me will take Fanty an' ride hard fer the Double C Ranch,' said Lofty. 'I guess your Uncle Septimus won't waste no time a-seekin' out the killers who's pretendin' ter be Double C cowboys. As fer you, pardners,' added Lofty, 'Little Cloud will go at Indian pace—t'ain't runnin' an' t'ain't walkin'—it's kind of betwixt an' between. An' you gotta keep up with him— don't fall behind, or he'll think you're weaklin's . . .'

The two boys leaped for the door of the cabin as Little Cloud streaked out into the early sunlight and they trotted behind him along the faint track, among the sand and rocks and thorn-bushes, off into the narrow valley that wound between the yellow rocks of the hills to the distant Moccasin encampment.

Meanwhile Fanty the elephorse had been saddled. The two cowboys mounted and, before setting out for the Double C Ranch, took a last long look after Little Cloud and his hostages.

'Wal,' drawled Lefty, 'them boys is on their own now. They asked fer an adventure an' they sure gettin' it.

44

You reckon they kin stand up to Injun torture, if they hev to?'

'I reckon they kin,' said Lofty. 'There's only one thing that worries me . . . supposin' they was to reach the Injun camp and Little Cloud couldn't speak fer them? What would the Injuns do to them, seein' their shirt with the Double C badges—the brand o' the outfit they think been attackin' them?'

'But thet's crazy talk, pardner!' objected Lefty. 'They got Little Cloud with them, ain't they? Little Cloud will say why they're along with him . . . why shouldn't he?'

'Supposin' Little Cloud *warn't* there? Supposin' they reached the Moccasin camp without him? Supposin' Little Cloud got . . . *killed*!'

'But thet's crazy!' scoffed Lefty, 'Who's a-goin' ter attack an Injun youngster like Little Cloud?'

'The evil spirit they call the Curse of the Moccasins would,' answered Lofty. 'The spirit they call the Slayer of Braves . . . the Eater of Chiefs . . . the *Ugudugu-djuk*, pardner, which is the Moccasin word for the Thing that Travels Beneath the Earth.

'Suppose,' Lofty went on, 'suppose the *Ugudugu-djuk* is up there on the valley trail—lyin' awaitin' ter destroy Little Cloud?'

CHAPTER 11

GO SEEK THE ZOGA!

WHEN it came to keeping up with Little Cloud, David and Toby were very soon in difficulties. You couldn't say he was running, yet you couldn't say he was walking—certainly not as the cowboys walked. anyway. They kept their knees apart, as if they were still astride a horse, and they swung one hip forward and then the other, with their hands on the butts of their six-shooters.

But Little Cloud seemed just to glide over the ground without disturbing the sand, although David and Toby, toiling along behind him, moved in a constant haze of choking dust.

They left the creek far behind. They plodded along, sometimes weaving among great patches of thorn bush and cactus and sometimes scrambling over loose rock and great boulders, as Little Cloud moved gradually from the plain towards the craggy ridge of the hills. As the sun rose higher, the day became fiercely hot. The boys tipped their hats over their eyes, pulled up their scarves over their noses to keep out the dust, and panted after the Indian.

By noon the distance between them and Little Cloud began to widen. Toby, being the younger, felt the strain more and David took his hand to help him along— although he would dearly have liked someone to help *him* along too.

'When do we get to Moccasin camp, Little Cloud?' he called.

And the young brave answered, without looking back, 'Little Cloud get there before sundown . . .'

'Which means we can jolly well look after ourselves,' muttered David.

'I don't think I can keep this up for very long,' Toby panted.

'We *have* to,' said David. 'We've got to show we can do as well as he can , , , or nearly as well, anyway.'

But now Toby was getting what his mother used to call his 'mutinous look'. He stuck his bottom lip out and began to say a few angry things about Little Cloud.

'He's just an old window-sneaker-in-atter,' he said bitterly.

'He's a *what*?' asked David.

'You know what I mean,' said Toby. 'He's a stack in the babber . . . he's a . . . a . . . a ride on the hoofer.' Toby pulled his hand away from David and began to plunge ahead, still talking angrily. 'Little Cloud big brave, ha! Bet if he was in Dingle Down on market day and he saw old Farmer Prosser's bull he'd run a mile, wouldn't he, David? Yes, he would,' said Toby, answering his own question and pounding on so that David had to put on a spurt to keep up with him. 'And I bet he'd scream his head off if he saw a Troll. Why, I bet he's scared of us. I bet he's only trying to keep away from us. Come on, David, let's get in front of him and make *him* hurry to keep up for a change.' And Toby, whose anger seemed to have taken his tiredness away, set off at a run, with David labouring after him.

They came to within a couple of yards of Little Cloud, just as the Indian was rounding a huge rock, when Toby suddenly shouted, 'Get a move on, Very Little Cloud, we're going to race you!' They saw Little Cloud falter a moment and turn his head toward them. And as he did so a look of terror came into his face anl with a wild shriek he vanished from their sight.

'I told you he was scared of us,' shouted Toby. 'Come on, David . . .'

But David grabbed his arm to try to get him to stop. 'It's not us he's frightened of,' cried David. 'There must be something else . . .' At that moment they turned the corner by the rock—and what they saw brought them both, horrified, to a halt.

For there, slowly sinking into the ground, as though he was being sucked down by some irresistible force, was Little Cloud. The earth below him heaved as if some monstrous creature was below, clawing him down to his death. But the really frightening thing was that Little Cloud was not fighting to free himself: his arms were folded and only the tightness of his lips showed the terror that he must be feeling.

As he saw the two boys he raised his left arm and cried, 'Farewell, little Chiefs! Ugudugu-djuk, Slayer of Braves, is taking Little Cloud to his wigwam. Tell Chief Bald Eagle Little Cloud died bravely.'

'We can't leave him like this,' cried David. And even as he spoke Little Cloud sank further, almost to his waist. 'Come on, then,' shouted Toby, 'but keep on the firm ground. We'll each grab an arm.'

They dashed forward and bent all their strength to

47

freeing Little Cloud from the grip of the Thing below. They panted and pulled and dug in their heels but the most they seemed able to do was to keep Little Cloud from being drawn down any further into the ground.

'If only he'd try to help himself,' muttered David, as he felt his own strength failing.

At that moment the Indian suddenly panted, 'Little Cloud's feet free.' And hope came back into his face. 'Ugudugu-djuk no longer want to eat young brave. Pull, Little Chiefs!' And with one great, final effort, the boys dragged Little Cloud on to firm ground and there they all lay, panting.

Then—'Look!' said Toby. For a strange ridge of earth was moving away from the road. It was as if some great burrowing animal had come a little too near the surface and was forcing the roof of its tunnel above the ground. As they watched they saw the ridge moving away up the hillside, winding in and out among the boulders.

'You save Little Cloud from Ugudugu-djuk,' said the Indian, and as they turned towards him, David and Toby saw that his moccasins were gone and that the legs of his deerskin trousers had been ripped as though by massive claws.

'We must get you back to camp as quickly as possible,' said David. 'Can you walk, Little Cloud?'

'Little Cloud walk—but slowly,' said the Indian, rising painfully to his feet. 'Hear me. Let my brothers seek among rocks for little plant with yellow leaves—so big,' and he pointed to the nail on his little finger. 'On leaves is black cross. Perhaps no luck—but seek one hour. If find, bring leaf.'

Little Cloud set off on the trail. David and Toby separated, David taking one side of the track and Toby the other. After the exertions of the morning, it was almost restful to roam about among the boulders, pausing now and then to study some scrubby, thorny little plant in the hope of seeing a tiny, yellow leaf . . . even one. But it seemed a hopeless search.

'I wonder if Little Cloud thought this up to give us

a rest?' said Toby to himself. 'It doesn't seem half as hard as plodding along the trail and we *are* making some progress. Looking around like this keeps my mind occupied at any rate.' And with that he tripped over a big stone and would have come a cropper if his foot had not loosened the stone from the ground and sent it rolling to one side.

Toby just managed to keep his balance and looked down to see what had tripped him. And there, on the very edge of the hole where the stone had been, and hidden until then by its shadow, was a tiny little plant smothered in small yellow leaves. Toby flung himself down and peered closely at them. Sure enough, each leaf bore the black cross that Little Cloud had told them to look for. Excitedly Toby stripped the plant and stuffed his pocket with the leaves. His cry of 'I've got it!' brought David scrambling back and together they joined Little Cloud.

Toby pushed a leaf into his hand. 'Is that what you want, Little Cloud?' he asked, and knew, as he saw the Indian's eyes light up, that he had been right.

'My brothers save Little Cloud's life. Also bring much good fortune,' said Little Cloud gravely. 'Only one day in whole year is leaf on Zoga plant,' he said. 'Only one Zoga plant in many miles. Now behold what Zoga leaf can do! Very powerful. Eat only little.' He broke the tiny leaf with his nail into three little pieces. Putting one between his lips he handed the other two to David and Toby.

'Eat, my brothers,' said Little Cloud. 'Eat. Walk. Soon Zoga power work for us.'

The sun was now very low and the air was growing bitterly cold. Little Cloud had meant to be at the Moccasin encampment before the light faded, but with the delay and his injuries, that must be impossible, for there were miles to go and the strain was beginning to tell on the two boys. They plodded slowly beside Little Cloud and chewed on the little piece of tasteless yellow leaf listlessly and unbelievingly.

Then suddenly Toby said, 'Ooh!'

And David said, 'What?' and almost at the same moment, he cried, 'Ooh!' as well.

And Little Cloud, for the first time since they had met him, seemed so pleased that he came very near to smiling—which is something that Indians hardly ever do. 'What happened, my brothers?' he asked.

'Why, I bounced!' exclaimed Toby.

'So did I!' said David. 'I just seemed to spring up in the air. Look, it's happening again.'

'I feel I don't weigh anything at all!' said Toby.

'Zoga make you light as feather,' said Little Cloud. 'Come—we race sun.' He seized their hands, crying, 'Run, brothers, run!'

And they all ran. How they ran! Their feet seemed not to touch the ground but to skim over it. It was almost like flying. All their weariness had gone. Right up the hill they sped in the dying light until . . . it seemed almost a matter of minutes . . . they found themselves looking down on the Indian encampment. Little Cloud halted them all suddenly and peered searchingly at the scene below: a blazing camp fire and a host of seated Indians.

And then, 'Come, my brothers, come!' cried Little Cloud, urgently, starting forward. 'Faster, faster!' There was cold fear in his voice. 'Faster, brothers! *I smell treachery!*' And they flew like a wild wind from the mountains down, down to the Moccasin camp.

CHAPTER 12

WHAT HAPPENED TO HUNTER OF THE MOON

THE first thing they saw, as they neared the Indian encampment, was the huge totem pole, towering high above the tall wigwams, with its weird carvings of strange beasts and birds lit by the leaping flames of the blazing campfire.

Little Cloud and his companions seemed to skim over the crowd of seated braves into the space before the campfire, and they stopped facing the tall figure of the Indian Chief, halted in his speech by their sudden arrival. It was Chief Bald Eagle himself, in his magnificent headdress of eagle feathers that fell right to the ground. He had a great beaky nose and his bronzed face was wrinkled with age—but from that face keen black eyes still flashed fearlessly.

As the three came to a halt before him he showed no trace of surprise. He raised his arm to still the murmuring among the crowd of braves and said, 'Speak now, Little Cloud. Tell how you killed cowboys of Double C and how you captured young Cobwebb braves.'

Then Little Cloud replied in a loud voice, 'Hear me. Little Cloud went out to kill. He has not killed. He has not come back bringing enemies of Moccasins, but with his brothers.'

This was news the Indians had never expected. A great hubbub broke out. There were shouts of anger. Tomahawks and scalping knives were brandished. But never a trace of emotion showed on the lined face of Chief Bald Eagle. He threw up both his arms and every voice was silent.

In a cold voice Bald Eagle said, 'Moccasins will judge when they know all. Speak on, Little Cloud.'

And, with a hand on the shoulder of each of the boys, Little Cloud told the tribe everything. He told how he had been captured by Fanty—he called him the Horse whose Nose is a Snake. He told how he had been disarmed, how his captors had denied that Chief Cobwebb of the Double C Ranch would ever break his faith with the Moccasins. He described how David and Toby—'young Chiefs of Cobwebb tribe'—had agreed to come as hostages, as proof of good faith. And he told also how the cowboys had freed him from his bonds and given him back his knife. And finally, he described his seizure by the Ugudugu-djuk, during the journey to rejoin his tribe, and how the boys had rescued him from death.

51

There was a great sigh from the vast crowd of braves as he finished, and then a long silence while all looked toward Chief Bald Eagle and waited for his words. At last he spoke.

'Little Chiefs of Cobwebb tribe,' he said, 'do you say your Chief has not broken pipe of peace with Moccasins?'

'We do,' answered David. And Toby, who was suddenly feeling hungry, and consequently was once again in a bad temper, snapped, 'Of course we do. Why d'you think we came as hostages?'

'And this was agreed before the sun rose this day?' asked Chief Bald Eagle relentlessly.

'Yes,' answered David, and Toby grunted fiercely.

'They have spoken,' said the Chief. and he turned to the young brave. 'And Little Cloud believe this?' he asked.

'Yes,' said Little Cloud stoutly.

The old Chief spread his arms wide. 'Let Little Cloud look well among all the tribe before him,' he said. 'Let him say if he sees the face of Hunter of the Moon, great Medicine Man of the Moccasins.'

Little Cloud gazed at the great concourse of braves and said at length. 'I do not see him.'

'And now,' cried Chief Bald Eagle in ringing tones, 'I will tell Little Cloud why he does not see Medicine Man here. He does not see him because one hour ago— many hours after Chief Cobwebb's cowboys gave us second pledge of peace and sent these hostages—one hour ago Hunter of the Moon was ambushed and killed . . .' Chief Bald Eagle paused dramatically, and then he added, *'and when we found him, Little Cloud, there was a mark upon his forehead. It was brand of the Double C.'*

David and Toby felt as if they had lost all power to speak or move. There was horror in the eyes of Little Cloud. A great silence, more menacing than the previous angry shouting, hung over the great arena. The tribe was waiting for Chief Bald Eagle to speak the words of judgment.

'We ask,' said the Chief, at last, 'if these young Chiefs speak straightly or with forked tongues? Have they come as hostages or as spies? Bald Eagle must know truth. Hear me!'

There was a great stir among the crowd. The verdict was now to be given.

'This night,' said Chief Bald Eagle, 'young Chiefs of Double C will rest in wigwam of Hunter of the Moon. May his spirit question them and speak to us through the Totem. If the tribe has had no answer by time tomorrow's sun is half-way across the sky, then they will be put to torture. I have spoken.'

Silently the huge crowd fell back, to give the boys passage to the dead man's wigwam. Little Cloud made a movement as if to walk beside them, but Bald Eagle waved him imperiously away.

Two warriors stepped forward to seize them, but David, grabbing Toby's hand, turned fiercely on them. 'Get back!' he cried. 'We can walk there without help. Come on, Toby.'

But Toby had something to say, too. He was hungry, and when Toby gets hungry, he gets hopping mad. This time, to make his anger worse, he had just caught a whiff of a most meaty and delicious stew from the Moccasins' cooking pots.

'Little Cloud,' he snapped, 'tell Chief Bald Eagle that Double C cowboys *feed* their captives. *They're* not mean!'

And David and Toby stalked off together towards the dark doorway of the Medicine Man's wigwam and the grim ordeal that lay before them.

CHAPTER 13

THE MUSIC OF THE HAIRY ONE

WHAT Toby had said must have made Bald Eagle feel very mean indeed, because just as the boys were about to enter the Medicine Man's wigwam, he snapped an order and a squaw shuffled over to hand them each a bowl of steaming stew. Once they were inside the tent, the cover of hides was drawn together and laced tight and two braves squatted on guard outside, holding their tomahawks in their laps. The only light inside the wigwam came from the moonlight that filtered in from the smoke outlet at the top and from a twist of cotton burning feebly in a tiny bowl of oil.

David and Toby sat on the pile of soft, warm animal skins that covered the floor of the wigwam and not a word was spoken as they spooned up the savoury stew. Finally, with a long 'Aaah!' Toby put down his bowl and said, rather worriedly, 'David . . . do *you* think the g-ghost of Hunter of the Moon might c-come and question us tonight?'

David, who had been expecting this and was feeling very uneasy himself said, boldly, 'No. It's all nonsense. Bald Eagle was only trying to scare us.'

'Oh,' said Toby. But he didn't feel very happy.

'Yes,' said David, trying to be much braver than he felt. 'It's like Lofty told us . . . they're only trying to frighten us. We mustn't let them. At least,' he added hastily, 'if what they do *does* make us feel frightened, we mustn't show it. We mustn't cry out.'

'But it . . . it's awful just sitting here,' answered Toby in a shaky voice. 'We can't just sit here . . . w-w-waiting.'

'What else *can* we do?' asked David.

'W-w-well,' said Toby, 'couldn't we sing, or something?'

'I suppose we could,' said David, 'but it ought to be something cheerful—something that the Indians can tell is cheerful, even if they don't understand any of the words.'

'Yes,' said Toby, getting really interested in the idea, 'we ought to sing one of those Irish reel things . . . like that one called Phil the Fluter's Ball . . .'

'But I don't know the words of that,' David objected.

'Neither do I,' said Toby, 'but I know the tune. The words don't matter. It's a really good, lively tune. It goes like this—come on—' And he began to sing.

Dum doodle dum, doodle doodle doodle dum—
Dum dumble do, doodle doodle dumble dee.
Oh, dum doodle dum, doodle doodle doodle dum
Doodle oodle oodle oodle oodle fumble umble ee.

So, making up nonsense words as they went along, David and Toby sang away at the tops of their voices. They sang and sang and they were just about forgetting their fears when . . .

Dum doodle dum doodle, David, look at that!
sang Toby. And David answered, still singing:
Dum dumble do, Yes, I see it, but sing on!
Their voices quavered quite a bit and the melody went a little shaky, but they went on bravely as they watched the amazing thing that was happening in the centre of the wigwam.

For the great pile of animal pelts was heaving and rising from the ground. And as they gazed, horrified, but still faltering along with their song, the furs fell apart and revealed a blood-chilling sight.

Coming up from a hole in the ground was a great hairy head, a head covered with long grey silky hair that hid all the face except where there peeped out the tip of a round nose! You could just see the gleam of the eyes in the feeble light of the oil lamp, but it was impossible to make out where the mouth was or where the chin ended, for as the figure rose further from the hole, the boys saw that the hair over the face hung down to mingle with that of the broad hairy chest. Two huge hairy arms were next drawn up from the earth and the figure spread its elbows on each side of the hole and rested on them. The boys saw that the vast hairy hands bent inwards from the wrist and that the nails were inches long and like huge steel talons!

With all this going on right in front of them, you can understand why the voices of David and Toby became more and more shaky. They had nearly failed altogether when the Hairy One suddenly plunged a hand under its fur . . . *and the next moment the wild notes of a violin rang out in the very tune they were trying to sing.*

*This horrible apparition is the first sight that David and
Toby had of Mr Murphy. He was called Paddy Murphy
because his first names were Patrick Aloysius Demosthenes, which is quite understandable, isn't it?*

The music was gay and jolly and the boys forgot to be frightened as it carried them along. They sang verse after verse of nonsense words and the music grew faster and faster until they just could not keep pace with it. Then, with a wild, hilarious screech, the violin stopped, leaving David and Toby panting and laughing ... yes, actually laughing.

At that moment a voice broke from the Hairy One. 'Wait till I get me nails trimmed, me bhoyos,' it said, 'an' I'll play it ever faster. But now, if ye don't mind me making meself at home, 'tis Bald Eagle himself we'll serenade. By the long white beard av McGinty's goat, 'tis me ould violin that'll make him think there's a whole regiment av screamin's ghosts in this wigwam.'

And once again the violin began. But this time the notes were shrill and weird. Then they changed to a deep groaning, then to a shouting, a screeching. Then the player would make his instrument speak with the tongues of animals: the whinny of a frightened horse, the scream of an eagle, the eerie, distant yapping of a pack of prairie dogs.

At first the boys could hear voices raised in fear from the Indian camp outside. Then there was silence, as if the Moccasins had shut themselves up in their wigwams. The last sound of all from outside the wigwam of Hunter of the Moon was a shuffle and a sudden strangled cry as the two Indian braves guarding their prisoners finally lost their nerve and fled, babbling that the spirit of the dead Medicine Man was pursuing them.

Then the music suddenly stopped. The Hairy One put down its violin, heaved its hairy legs into sight and sat on the floor with its feet dangling in the hole.

'I knew that little overture would scare the Moccasins into their wigwams,' it said. 'And now, me bhoyos, we can talk in peace, so as we get ourselves introduced. I heard you speakin', just before I came in. The bigger boy—you'll be David? And you're Toby?—'

'And what's your name, Mr ... er ... er ...?' put in Toby, who couldn't wait a moment longer.

'Me?' said the Hairy One. 'Why now, have ye not guessed already? I'm the Curse of the Moccasins, the Slayer of Braves, the Eater of Chiefs, the Thing that Travels Beneath the Earth. In fact, I'm the Ugudugudjuk . . . *But back in dear ould Oireland,*' he added, *'me mother calls me Paddy Murphy.'*

CHAPTER 14

THE KILLERS UNMASKED

'THEN it was you, Mr Murphy,' said David sternly, 'it was you who tried to kill Little Cloud yesterday on the track through the hills . . .'

'Little Cloud's the son of Bald Eagle, the Moccasin Chief,' put in Toby, 'and he's our friend. We managed to save him from you when you were trying to pull him down under the ground,' he added angrily. 'What do you want to go around killing people for?'

'But I *don't!*' protested Paddy Murphy, the hair that covered his mouth blowing up and down as he spoke. 'Why, me heart's as warm as a kettle on th' boil and the milk av human kindness is nearly runnin' out av me ears. I never kilt a man in me life. All I ever done,' said Mr Murphy earnestly, 'has been to take me tunnels under the feet av an Injun when I needed a new pair av moccasins or when me trousers were worn out. Clothin' perishes terrible quick when a man's makin' a tunnel. See this pair o' shorts? They were a full-length pair o' trousers only a week ago. And the moccasins I got from your friend Little Cloud yesterday were worn to ribbons in a few hours av kickin' away the earth behind me during the tunnellin' . . .'

'Do you mean to say you actually *live* underground?' said David in amazement. 'All the time, I mean?'

'Indeed I do,' said Paddy Murphy, sadly. 'I *have* to do.'

'But what about food?' said Toby.

'And water?' added David.

'And what do you do when you're *not* making tunnels?' asked Toby eagerly.

'Ah, now, me bhoyos, one thing at a time!' protested Mr Murphy. 'In the beginning, for that's the right place to start a story—in the beginning I was prospectin' for gold with a partner. Well, one day my partner was shot. The blame was put on me. I knew what kind of man did the killin' but I didn't know his name. If I could keep meself from being caught, I might be able to track him down. But that meant staying near the very people who were huntin' me. There was only one way to do that—I went underground—really underground. Who would think of lookin' beneath the earth for me? Who would think that Paddy Murphy could have turned himself into a human mole?'

'But about food . . .?' prompted David.

'Ah, yes, food and water and so on. Well, now, me bhoyos, just consider this: in places like here, for instance, where there's few streams, the sun can fry you during the day yet the nights can be freezin' cold. But under the ground it's neither too hot nor too cold. Up above it can be dusty and dry, with scarcely a green plant growing. Down below there's no dust and instead of thorny plants and cactuses full of prickles, there's only the nice juicy roots for Paddy Murphy to harvest for his meals. Up above you can even die of thirst. But Paddy Murphy digs his tunnels down to the rock where the water gathers deep under the ground. And Paddy Murphy can move about unseen both by day and by night. He can hear what's said in the ranch-house and what's whispered in the wigwam. And so, sooner or later, Paddy Murphy will be able to prove who it was that murdered his partner and hand that man over to justice.'

This sounded a pretty good explanation of Paddy Murphy's activities but David was still not satisfied.

'But if you take only the Indians' shoes and clothing, Mr Murphy,' he said, 'how is it they call you the Killer of Braves, the Eater of Chiefs and that sort of thing? The Indians who call you this are braves, they are warriors. Why should they say you're so terribly frightening? . . . that is, if it's really true that you haven't killed any of them?'

Mr Murphy's reply to this was a long deep chuckle. Then he said, 'Well now, David me bhoyo, suppose I put it like this. If you were an Indian brave and you came back to the camp and you said, *"I have just been attacked by the terrible, deadly Ugudugu-djuk. It has the strength of ten men and huge claws and it came out of the earth and tried to kill me. But I, great Indian warrior, fought with it and beat it off so that it ran away. Look at my clothing, ripped and torn by its steely claws."* Well now,' went on Paddy Murphy, 'if you came back with a story like that, everybody would think how brave you were even to get away from such a terrible enemy!

'But suppose now,' he added, 'the same Indian brave came back to camp and he said, *"Paddy Murphy pulled me into a hole in the ground and pinched me trousers."* Well,' said Mr Murphy, as David and Toby burst out laughing, 'you can understand why they make me out to be so terrible! . . . However, perhaps you wouldn't mind answering a question that Paddy Murphy has in *his* mind. How come you two boys to be here?'

So they told him the whole story and Mr Murphy thought it over for a while. Then he said, 'You can escape right now—I can lead you to safety through my tunnels.'

But David said, 'But then the Indians may think we've run away and that will make them all the more certain that it was the cowboys from the Double C Ranch that attacked them.'

'You mean you're goin' to face the threat of torture when you could get clean away?' gasped Mr Murphy, in amazement. David looked at Toby and Toby took a deep breath and said, 'I think we just *have* to, Mr Murphy.'

'Well, I won't press you,' he answered, 'but I promise you I'll be pretty close at hand to see if the Moccasins start anything like that. And if they do—by the long white beard of McGinty's goat, the Ugudugu-djuk will get them before they can do any harm to you!'

The boys felt very much happier when they heard this and they thanked their mole-like friend.

'Now, before I go back underground,' said Mr Murphy, 'I wonder if you'd be so kind as to look round the wigwam and see if there's anything like a pair of moccasins lying about, or any usable clothing. I'll take one or two skins. I can sew them up to make a stout pair of trousers, but it's something for me poor feet I really need most.'

The boys rooted about among the piles of skins but all that they brought into the glow of the tiny lamp at last was a shirt and one leather boot. Mr Murphy shook out the shirt to see if it was big enough. Then suddenly he cried, 'But what's a shirt with the Double C mark on it doing here?'

David said, 'Quick, Toby, hand me that boot!' He turned it round in the light. 'Look,' he said, 'there's a Double C mark on this too!'

'I know,' said Toby excitedly. 'These are the things that the Moccasins said they found after the cowboy attack—the things that proved it was the Double C cowboys who had broken the pipe of peace.'

There was a long silence. Then Paddy Murphy said, 'Since I'm most of the time below ground, perhaps my eyes can see better than yours in this light. It seems to me that those brands are not the same as the ones you have on your shirts.'

David and Toby looked closely at their own brand marks, sewn on their shirts, and they were like those at the top of the next page.

Then they looked at the marks on the captured shirt and boot and they seemed really hardly any different at all. They were like this:

'I think the only difference is that those have been badly sewn on,' said David at last. 'I mean, whoever sewed them on has turned the piece of material in too much at one side.'

'Then we'll cut the brand mark off that boot,' said Paddy Murphy, 'and see just what it looks like when it's opened out.'

Frankly, David and Toby felt he was making a great mystery out of nothing. But then, with his dagger-like nails, Mr Murphy ripped away the threads that held down the piece of cloth with the brand mark of the Double C and opened it out flat, close to the flickering flame of the lamp.

'There now, me bhoyo's he said quietly, 'what d'ye make of that?'

For the brand was no longer that of the Double C but this:

'It's an O!' exclaimed David, bewildered.

'But what does it mean, Mr Murphy?' asked Toby.

'It means that we now know who *really* has been attacking the Moccasins,' answered Paddy Murphy. 'That's the brand of the Big O outfit—the worst gang of desperadoes in the West. The Double C Ranch will want 'em brought to justice. And so do I, me bhoyos, for one of 'em is the man that killed my partner. From now on, the Slayer of Braves, the Eater of Chiefs, the Ugudugu-djuk—in fact, me bhoyos, Paddy Murphy himself will join in the hunt!'

CHAPTER 15

THE MYSTERIOUS CHIMNEY

'It would be wonderful, wouldn't it, Toby?' said David eagerly, 'if we could track down the ringleaders of the Big O outfit and capture them without the help of Uncle Septimus or the Moccasins!'

Toby agreed. 'But,' he said, 'if we vanish from the camp through Mr Murphy's tunnels, the Moccasins will think we've sneaked off because we really *are* spies and then they may go on the warpath against Uncle Septimus. I wish we *could* go after the Big O on our own, though, but I'm afraid it's impossible.'

'Impossible!' exclaimed Paddy Murphy. 'Why, me bhoyos, I admit no such word in my philosophery. An' whenivver I'm tempted to use that disgustful expression, I turn for strength to the inspirin' history av Paddy McGinty's goat.'

Producing his violin from under his thick fur, he put it to his shoulder and began to play and sing:

He could chew up any ropes—he could bite through any chains,
For McGinty's was a goat that knew just how to use his brains.
When they locked him in the prison, swearin' he'd escape no more—
Why, he simply put his head to work—and butted down the door.

'Which goes to prove,' added Mr Murphy, as his violin vanished again under his fur, 'that there's nothing a man can't do if he'll only use his head. So let me stimulerate the ould brain.'

He began to scratch his head and scratch his head until his hair stuck out all ways, giving him a more frightening appearance than ever. At last he said, 'Glory be, I see a ray av light! Listen, me bhoyos. If the Moccasins left this wigwam fastened up for a month— for your friends of the Double C won't come looking for you before that time, as they agreed—well then, that would give us time to track down the killers ourselves, and . . .'

'But how *can* we keep the Indians out of the wigwam!' exclaimed David, exasperated.

'They're coming for us at midday tomorrow to take us out and perhaps torture us,' added Toby.

'I don't think they will,' chuckled Paddy Murphy. 'Not if you're as wise as McGinty's goat. Now come close and I'll tell you my plan.'

The two boys listened eagerly to Paddy's idea.

Finally David said, 'It sounds marvellous, Mr Murphy, but are you sure it will work?'

'Of course I'm not *sure*,' cried Paddy Murphy, 'but ye nivver know what ye can do till ye try—as Pegeen O'Flaherty's hen said when she laid a 16-ounce egg!'

So the scheme was approved—after one small change. This was due to Toby, because when Paddy suggested they set the plan working first thing in the morning, Toby looked very pained and said, 'What before we've had anything to eat?' So Paddy agreed that first he would make a short tunnel and take some pemmican from the Moccasin's meat store. (Pemmican is minced-up buffalo meat that has been dried in the sun and it's awfully chewy. If you keep telling yourself that it's very nourishing, you may be able to forget the taste.) When the details were finally settled, they all lay down to snatch a few hours' sleep before day came.

It seemed only a few minutes before sunlight was filtering through the fastenings of the wigwam and the bustle and noise of a new day began in the Moccasin encampment. When David and Toby woke, Mr

Murphy had already made his underground trip and brought some pemmican—which was a good job because the hours wore on without any sign that the Indians were going to provide any breakfast at all for their hostages.

Finally, just before midday, Mr Murphy declared: 'Now's the time to get movin', me bhoyos. Follow me!' He began to slide down the hole in the middle of the wigwam. 'Now hand me the little oil-lamp,' he said, 'and last man down pull the skins over the top o' the hole.' Down he went. Toby followed him, then David.

It was an eerie sensation, clinging to the sides of the shaft, and going inch by inch lower and lower. Then, from below them, they heard the voice of Paddy Murphy. 'The shaft comes into a small cave through the roof. When you feel nothin' beneath your feet, just let go and drop.'

It was not a long drop, for the cave in which they landed was quite small—in fact, Mr Murphy had to kneel. In the dim light of the little lamp, they could see a hole, shaped like a doorway. It led into a wide, circular space that seemed to be the bottom of a chimney.

'Inside there,' said Mr Murphy, nodding towards the 'chimney', 'you'll find the point where my tunnel came in. I came across here when I heard Chief Bald Eagle say he was puttin' you in the wigwam up above. Not bad navigatin', though I say it meself. I was right under his feet when he was talking. 'Twas a sore temptation to pull him into the ground, tickle his feet, and then help meself to the old Chief's fancy moccasins.

'And now,' added Mr Murphy, 'would you young fellers like to climb a little way up that chimney? No difficulty, there are footholds all the way up. You'll find some holes in the side o' the shaft. Take a look through and tell me what you see.'

David crawled into the shaft, with Toby close behind him. As they looked upwards, they could see pale gleams of daylight here and there, as if the huge shaft had been pierced in places for ventilation.

C

Up they climbed. Then: 'Look, Toby!' cried David.

And Toby answered, 'I'm looking! Let's get higher and then we'll have a better view.'

'Mr Murphy,' called David, 'what is this place? Where are we?'

Paddy Murphy answered with a chuckle, 'You're inside the great Totem pole in the middle of the Moccasin camp. Look for the Chief's wigwam and tell me what you see.'

David scanned the encampment, then he called excitedly, 'They've set up two poles, near the Chief's wigwam, and there are great piles of faggots all round them!'

And Toby took up the tale. 'A group of braves have come up to Bald Eagle's wigwam. Now Chief Bald Eagle is coming out. He's pointing to the poles where the faggots are laid. Now he's pointing to Hunter of the Moon's wigwam—*our* wigwam. And now they're all marching towards it. *Mr Murphy! Mr Murphy!! They're coming to take us to the torture!*

CHAPTER 16

BY ORDER OF THE TOTEM

'THEN the time has come for action,' declared Mr Murphy in reply. 'Move a bit higher, me bhoyos, and let me come aloft.' He clambered up behind them and wedged himself comfortably in the shaft near one of the openings. 'Now let you be silent,' he went on, 'and leave the rest to me and me fiddle.'

David and Toby looked down on the Indian encampment. Coming nearer and nearer to the Totem pole and the wigwam of Hunter of the Moon was Chief Bald Eagle, walking with slow and solemn steps. Behind him was Little Cloud, with sadness in his face, and following him a group of the tribe's leading warriors. In a great arc behind them, and at a respectful distance, were the young braves, the boys still untried in conflict, and behind them again were the squaws and the young girls.

And now Bald Eagle was in the shadow of the Totem pole, with its grinning open-mouthed masks of strange beasts and birds representing the gods of the Moccasins. Now he had stopped and the retinue of braves moved closer as he bent forward and stretched his hand to unloose the leather thongs that kept the wigwam closed.

And at that moment the Totem spoke! Moans, shrieks and yells, like the wailing of tormented souls poured from its fearsome mouths!

Bald Eagle pulled back his hand as though he had had a violent electric shock and turned in awe towards the mighty Totem. Little Cloud turned with him. The band of seasoned warriors wavered for a moment, but kept their ranks. Behind them the great crowd of young braves, boys, squaws and girls melted away into the shelter of the wigwams.

Inside the wide, echoing shaft of the Totem, Mr Murphy sawed away at his violin and yelled, screeched and roared with it. The wooden walls magnified the awful sound and added strange echoes to it, till the whole shaft vibrated so much that Toby and David feared that at any moment they might be shaken down on top of their companion. Then, just as suddenly as it had begun, the noise stopped.

And then Paddy Murphy began to cry out, in a weird sort of moaning voice, 'Whoo-ooo! The gods would speak! Whoo-ooo! Let Chief Bald Eagle approach!'

Bald Eagle motioned his followers to stay where they were. He took off his huge headdress of black and white feathers and handed it to Little Cloud. Then he removed his moccasins.

'Did y'ever see the like?' whispered Paddy Murphy. 'The ould gentleman holds us in proper respect. Now just you watch while I give him his orders, me bhoyos.'

Bald Eagle came slowly to the foot of the huge

Totem pole. He stopped, knelt on the ground before it and bowed his head.

Then he said, very humbly, 'Bald Eagle listens, O spirits-who-must-be-obeyed.'

At this Mr Murphy began his whooo-oo-ing again and gave his commands. 'The spirit of Hunter of the Moon has joined the gods of the Moccasins. *Whoo-oo!* While the bodies of the young hostages sleep, he has brought their spirits to the gods for questioning. *Whoo-oo!* They will return after the space of one moon. *Whoo-oo!* Till then let no man enter the wigwam of Hunter of the Moon. It is guarded by the Ugudugu-djuk! The gods have spoken!' And with this, Paddy Murphy let out a yell that shook the huge Totem pole to its foundations.

In fact, it shook so violently that David lost his footing and fell on Toby and Toby lost his hold too. and they went down—whoosh!—on to the head of Paddy Murphy, and all three of them landed in a heap at the foot of the shaft with an echoing bump. They hadn't time to cry out, but it would not have mattered because Chief Bald Eagle was by now out of earshot and, arms held high, was delivering the message of the Totem to his people.

The boys and Mr Murphy unscrambled themselves and sat down panting in the little cave.

'Well now, me bhoyos,' said Mr Murphy at last, 'We've got the best part av a month to bring these desperadoes av the Big O Ranch to justice. It'll give me great joy ter see that evil man, Jabez Gunn, locked up in his own jail.'

'But who's Jabez Gunn?' asked David.

'Arrah, now, av course ye don't know,' said Paddy. 'Well, I'll have to go back to the time my partner was shot. He was able to tell me two things: the man who shot him was a man with a limp and he wore the Big O badge. Before I could get on his trail, Sheriff Gunn arrested me and accused me of killin' me own partner!'

'But didn't you tell him about the limping man?' asked Toby.

*Chief Bald Eagle bows before the great Totem pole to
listen to the message from the gods of the Moccasin tribe.
As a mark of respect he has taken off the great feathered
headdress and the embroidered cloak which form his
badge of office. The sign on his back is to make it clear
to the tribe, however, that he is still the man in charge.
Chief Bald Eagle never takes chances.*

'Av course I did,' answered Mr Murphy. 'But Sheriff Gunn happens to own the Big O Ranch and he said there was no limpin' man worked for him. And then he said somethin' else: he said that if I'd tell him where we'd found gold and hand over the claim to him, then he'd let me go. That made me believe that he was hand-in-glove with the killer. I asked him fer time to think it over and he gave me till next morning. That night I dug my way out av the jail and began my life as a sort av human mole.'

'Do you really own a gold mine, Mr Murphy?' asked Toby.

'I worked a mine, with me partner,' said Mr Murphy, 'but we never found any gold. I didn't tell that to Sheriff Gunn, though, fer I knew he meant to hang me anyway, to shield the real murderer.'

'But why are Sheriff Gunn and his gang making all these attacks on the Moccasins?' asked David.

'I'm sure that once again it's because of gold,' said Mr Murphy. 'There's a Moccasin legend that long ago that hill above their camp was full of gold and it all belonged to the tribe. Then the gods got angry with them and sent an earthquake and after it they were never able to find the gold again. The gods promised that one day they'd give the gold back to the tribe, and that's why they keep their camp in this desolate place— they're waiting for the Mountain of Gold to be opened up again. I've heard Jabez Gunn talking. He believes there's something in the story and he wants to find that lost gold mine. That would explain why he's trying to force the Moccasins to move away.'

'I see,' put in Toby excitedly, 'and he makes them think that Uncle Septimus is to blame so that the Indians will attack the Double C outfit . . .'

'. . . and while they're shooting each other,' David broke in, 'Gunn's men will move in and dig out the gold.'

'I reckon that's about the size of it,' said Mr Murphy. 'It's a dangerous man we have to tackle, me bhoyos— and a powerful man, too. Jabez Gunn is Sheriff of

70

Gopher City. Not only that—he's President av the Gopher City Bank, and he owns the Gopher City Saloon. What I suggest we do now is to take the tunnel to my underground headquarters and discuss our plans in comfort . . . But before we start, would you mind passin' me that ould shirt and the boot that had the Big O brand on it? One boot's better than none—and me own are worn out.'

David passed the things over and Paddy struggled into the shirt. Then he tried to put on the boot—but in vain. 'What's wrong with it?' he muttered. 'Is there something in it?' And he threw it down.

David picked up the boot and felt inside. Then he said, 'Tell me, Mr Murphy, did you ever see the limping man among the Big O cowboys?'

'I watched 'em many a time,' answered Mr. Murphy, 'but I never yet saw a limpin' man among 'em. So maybe my partner was wrong about that.'

'But he wasn't wrong!' cried David. 'Only by the time you got around to watching the Big O Cowboys, *the limping man didn't limp any more*. He'd had his right boot built higher inside to make his short leg as long as the other. This boot proves that the limping man exists!'

' 'Tis a masterly piece of deductification!' declared Mr Murphy admiringly. 'What are we waitin' for then? Follow me, me bhoyos! Into the tunnel—we're on the trail av the murderer!'

CHAPTER 17

IN THE SPIDER'S WEB

MR MURPHY dived into his tunnel. 'You go next, Toby,' said David, 'and I'll bring up the rear.' And off they went after Paddy.

It was a good job that Mr Murphy was so much bigger

than the two boys, because it made it much easier for them to crawl along behind him without banging their heads on the roof of the tunnel or catching their elbows on the rocks that often stuck out from the sides.

But it was very frightening in the complete darkness, with no sound except an occasional grunt from Mr Murphy, such as: 'Goin' down a bit here,' or 'Bearin' left now, me bhoyos.' And, of course, the two boys soon got tired of crawling. After all, they weren't used to it, and Paddy Murphy was. It became harder and harder to keep within hearing of his voice. They crawled on and on. Soon it seemed as if they had been underground for hours and hours. The tunnel went up and down, it turned this way and that, and eventually David and Toby were so weary that they couldn't spare any breath to talk to one another: they just plodded painfully along in silence, their knees and wrists aching terribly.

At length David felt he really must stretch a little to ease the pain. He raised his body and, *crack*!—he banged his head so hard on the rocky roof of the tunnel that he just had to stop and rest until the ache went away.

'Toby!' he called, as he prepared to set off again. There was no answer, so he called again, only louder. Still no answer. In fact, there was no sound at all. The tunnel was black and silent. And David realised what had happened. Somewhere in the darkness he had wandered into another tunnel, while his companions went on to Paddy Murphy's headquarters. He was alone and lost, deep under the earth!

David nearly panicked. He pulled out of his pocket the little bamboo tube that Lofty had given him in case he wanted to send an urgent message to Uncle Septimus. But then he realised that Lofty had not had time to tell him how to use it. 'I suppose I should blow through it,' David thought. 'But then, it can only be used once . . . and is this really an emergency? After all, this tunnel was probably made by Mr. Murphy and he knows where it is and where it goes. It must go somewhere. And when he and Toby find me missing, they'll come and find me.'

So he put the bamboo tube away again. He took off one boot and placed it in the middle of the tunnel with the toe pointing in the direction he was taking. Then he set off again in the darkness.

On and on he crawled. Once he found another small tunnel branching off to his left, but he kept straight ahead, leaving his other boot to mark the path he had taken. At length he felt a current of cool air, blowing down the tunnel. 'Thank goodness!' David said to himself. 'It seems to be coming out above ground so I'll be able to stand up and stretch at last!'

And then, some way ahead, he saw a yellowish, flickering light. Then he smelt woodsmoke. And then, as the tunnel brought him out into a small cave, he heard the crackle of flames and . . . men's voices.

Cautiously he stood up and peered from the cave. It was a clear, cold, starry night and there was a big white moon. A huge thornbush hid the entrance to the cave but beneath its branches he could see below him a sandy hollow sheltered by rocks. In the centre was a fire and, stretched at ease on the ground beside it, were two cowboys, deep in conversation. And on the shirt of each of them, clearly lit by the firelight, was the brand mark of the Big O outfit.

David strained his ears, but it was impossible to hear what the men were saying. He must get nearer. Trying to remember all he'd read about stalking, he crept out of the cave into the shelter of a boulder, and from there to another, a little lower. Then, quickly and silently, he made a dash across an open space and into cover again. Carefully he got to his feet to look out from his hiding place.

And at that moment, something dropped gently over his shoulders, and he found his arms pinioned tightly to his sides. There was a quick clatter of feet behind him. Below, the two cowboys had wheeled in his direction, kneeling with pistols ready. Then something cold was pressed against his neck and a voice snarled: 'Git

73

goin', tenderfoot . . . and no monkey tricks!' His captor gave a vicious jerk on the rope that bound him, and David stumbled down to the side of the fire.

'Waal,' drawled one of the cowboys mockingly as David came into the firelight, 'here's one o' the giants from the Double C outfit.'

'Yeah,' agreed the other, 'must be Lofty Cassidy's big brother. Better frisk him, Spider.'

David's captor passed an expert hand over him. 'No shootin' iron,' he commented, 'no money . . . nothin' 'cept this little tube of wood. Can't see what good it is but I guess I'll keep it, in case he was thinking of blowin' poisoned darts at us, eh, partners?'

He pushed David roughly to the ground and stood beside him. Looking up, David saw the face of the man called Spider—a narrow, evil face, thin-lipped and with eyes that seemed mere slits under the wide black hat.

'I spotted him among the rocks,' said Spider, jerking his head towards David. 'Guess he must ha' bin trailin' us fer hours.' Clearly he hadn't seen David come out of the cave, so Paddy Murphy's secret was in no danger yet.

'Waal, judgin' by the dirt on his clothes, he must ha' rolled all the way,' laughed one of the cowboys.

'He's a-goin' to tell us where he come from and why he's here,' said the man called Spider, 'and a lot of other things I want ter know. He can tell me while I'm gettin' my feet warm—and after that somebody else can go an' keep look-out.'

He began to kick off his boots and David saw with a shock of horror that without them his right leg was shorter than his left. Spider limped forward to take his seat beside the fire and as he did so, David, unable to stop himself, cried out, *'I know you! You're the man who killed Paddy Murphy's partner!'*

Taken completely by surprise, Spider snapped, 'How d'*you* know?' Then his hand flew to his revolver.

But already one of the other men had his gun in hand, pointing at Spider.

'Not here, Spider,' he said. 'We don't want ter know

74

nothin' about it. If you got accounts ter square with this young Cobwebb cowboy, take him way up the trail there—where we can't neither see nor hear what you're up to.'

Spider dragged his boots on in a fury. Then he jerked David to his feet and urged him away from the camp, up the trail and into the darkness.

It seemed as if, for David, the adventure was coming to a terrible end.

CHAPTER 18

THE SHADOW OF THE TROLLS

AND what was happening to Toby? Well, he had been very tired, too, crawling after Mr Murphy, and he was just about exhausted when at last he saw a glimmer of light at the end of the tunnel and he emerged in what Paddy called his headquarters.

And very comfortable headquarters they were, too. Toby found himself in a huge, round cave, high enough for even Paddy Murphy to stand up in comfort. It was lit by a great flame that came up through a hole in the floor and over this Mr Murphy had built a kind of shelf with a hole in it, just big enough to hold his coffee-pot which was already gurgling away when Toby crawled into the cave.

'Natural gas, me bhoyo,' crowed Mr Murphy, 'all me lightin' and all me cookin' and central heatin'—an' nothin' to pay!'

In another part of the cavern, cold sparkling water gushed from a spring into a deep rock basin, from which it ran away underground. Sleeping-places had been hollowed out in the walls and in these there were great cosy-looking piles of animal furs. Paddy Murphy had even carved out shelves in the wall as well and they were stacked with tins all neatly marked. There was *Coffee*, for instance, and *Indian Tea* and *Flour*. There were *Purple Cactus Root, Savoury Puffery Leaves* and other desert delicacies, side by side with odd things like *Snake Oil for Rheumatiz, Dynamite Sticks, Instant Buffalo Milk* and *Bunion Plasters*. And round the wall of the cave, at intervals, there were entrances to tunnels, all marked with their destinations—something like the passages you go down in London to the underground railway. Toby looked at them in turn. They read:

GOPHER CITY: For Sheriff Gunn's office, jail and cave overlooking Big O Ranch. (Toby supposed that was where Mr Murphy had kept watch when he was looking in vain for the limping man.)

MOCCASIN CAMP: For Chief Bald Eagle's wigwam and Indian hunting trails. (N.B. These trails is good spots for collecting moccasins and trousers.) Branch tunnel to Dead Man's Rocks.

GOOD GRUB CIRCLE: Goes by Purple Cactus plot, Puffery Shrub plantation, and best Google bushes around these parts. Northern branch to Jabez Gunn's chicken-coop.

The fourth tunnel was guarded by a heavy wooden door with a huge bar across it. And when Toby read the sign above this one, he jumped. For it said:

TROLL CHECK TUNNEL: (1) Keep this door closed when not in use.
(2) Never go down this tunnel without a shooting iron.
(3) Do not show a light at spy-hole.
(4) Check through spy-hole not less than once a week to see if Trolls are filtering back.
NEVER FORGET—ONE TROLL IS ONE TROLL TOO MANY!

'Mr Murphy!' cried Toby.
'Hold it, me bhoyo,' answered Paddy, who was bending over the stove. 'Coffee's comin' up and if you can

stay the pangs of hungerosity for another minute, there'll be pipin' hot Google-scones with it. Say, isn't it time your brother come out av the tunnel?'

'Oh, he'll be here in a minute or two,' said Toby impatiently. 'I want to know what that notice means over there. Are there really Trolls in these hills?'

'Nobody outside here knows it, me bhoyo,' answered Paddy Murphy, 'but a month or so ago I saw two of 'em. And straight away I sealed off that tunnel and set meself the job av keepin' watch. I have a spy-hole that looks down on a deep underground river. I think they travelled up that. They may pass on elsewhere but if they decide to settle here again and bring others, then I'll have to go warn the Moccasins and the people av Gopher City, even if Jabez Gunn catches me and hangs me. For Trools are evil, Toby lad, and when we had 'em here before, it took years to drive 'em out.'

'But what did they do?' asked Toby.

'They stole from everybody,' answered Paddy Murphy. 'They slithered into bedrooms at night and pinched people's toes off with their great big claws. They sliced through wigwam poles and brought the wigwams down on top of the people inside. They sidled across the trails in the darkness like great black crabs and carried embers from camp fires to set light to bunkhouses and the stables full of horses. Finally, cowboys and Indians together, we druv 'em out. They took off down Wailing River and that was the last we saw of 'em . . . until now. Look, me bhoyo,' added Mr Murphy, 'give that brother of yours a shout. He ought to be here by now.'

Well, Toby yelled down the tunnel, but as you know what had happened to David, you'll not be surprised by the fact that he got no answer. He shouted again and again. His fears grew. What was to be done?

CHAPTER 19

THIS WAY TO THE CIRCUS

PADDY MURPHY didn't seem unduly worried about David's disappearance. 'Just you give the scones a turn or two to get 'em brown,' he said, 'and I'll go back a way down the tunnel in case David fell asleep or somethin'.'

Mr Murphy dived into the darkness and he was gone quite a while. When at last he crawled into the cave, he said, 'Well, there's only one thing can have happened. David has got on the wrong track. He must have taken the branch tunnel that goes to Dead Man's Rocks...'

'Then we must go and find him,' said Toby. 'Come on, let's get going.'

'Arrah, now,' exclaimed Paddy 'will you stop and think a little? Look: when David finds the tunnel comes out into the open air, he'll realise he's taken the wrong turning. Being a sensible young feller, what will he do? I'll tell you. He'll either stay where he is at the end of the tunnel knowing I'll soon be after him, or he'll rest awhile and make his way slowly along the tunnel until he meets me a-looking for him. Am I not right, now?'

'Y-es,' Toby answered. 'I suppose you are. But ...'

'Av course I am,' said Paddy Murphy. 'Now, come have your coffee an' scones and let's plan. For I have an idea to talk over with you. It's about how to find the limpin' man.'

As they had their meal, Paddy unfolded his plan. It was that he should go to fetch David and meanwhile Toby should take the passage that came out at Gopher City. He would get there at dawn and after looking round the town, he would go to the shop of an old cowboy called One-Eye Joe.

'Now,' said Paddy, 'One-Eye Joe does all the boot repairs for the Big O outfit. You tell him you've been sent for some boots bein' repaired for . . . for . . . *"For who?"* says One-Eye. Then you say: *"Look, I'm a new boy workin' for the Big O and I clean forget his name . . . but his right leg is shorter than his left."* Well then, av course, old One-Eye says: *"Oh, you mean So-and-So,"* and he says his name. If he does have some boots there for the limpin' man, well, then it's all right. If he hasn't then you say the cowboys must have been havin' a joke with you. There, what d'you think of that?'

'It seems a jolly good idea,' Toby agreed.

'Sure, it's a good idea,' said Paddy Murphy heartily. 'Every time I have an idea I marvels at the profundicity av me intellect. The only real question I have in me mind about it is: will it work?'

Toby assured him that it certainly ought to work and then Paddy said it was time to set off. 'Me and David will follow you later,' he said, 'and we'll meet just inside the tunnel at the Gopher City end. I reckon you'll be there before we arrive. Good luck, me bhoyo—an' may we soon lay the murderer by the heels!'

It was a long, long journey through the tunnel and Toby took several naps on the way, since he wanted to feel really alert when it came to acting his part in front of the shoe-repairer.

At last he felt the tunnel rising sharply, and after some minutes of climbing he had a shock, for it seemed to come to a sudden end. However, Toby noticed that the soil was very loose so he supposed that there had been a collapse at the entrance to the tunnel. He scooped away with his hands and sure enough, in a minute or two he was able to poke a hand out and then, very cautiously, his head.

Now Paddy had told him that the tunnel came out behind a large bush close to the trail just outside Gopher City. But there was no bush there now. Instead Toby saw that near the exit from his burrow there was lying what appeared to be a huge pole. Then, as his eyes became accustomed to the light, he saw a very strange sight.

Some distance away was a long line of strange figures. In front of them was what looked like an enormously long roll of carpet and as Toby watched, bewildered, there was a sudden word of command and the strange figures began to push on this great roll. Suddenly, Toby realised that it was coming towards him. It was rolling across the sand at speed like a great grey tidal wave. He had hardly time to duck his head back into the tunnel when all daylight was blotted out as the huge grey mass swept over him.

Toby pushed up a hand and felt at the substance above his head. Then he sniffed. Then he sniffed again, for there was a smell he knew very well. And then, suddenly, he realised what had happened to him.

In a few moments the great pole beside him would be pulled into the air, lifting the great covering and . . . 'Good heavens!' gasped Toby. 'They're putting up a circus tent—*and I'm right in the middle of the ring!*'

CHAPTER 20

THE TERROR FROM THE SKY

Now we'd better get back quickly to David, who is plodding slowly up the trail beside Dead Man's Rocks with his arms tied to his sides by Spider's lasso and the barrel of the killer's revolver pressed against his back.

'Turn in among these rocks,' said Spider suddenly, and when they were well hidden from the trail he pushed David roughly to the ground.

'Set there,' he growled. 'Now I'm a-goin' ter set on this rock here with this shootin' iron aimed right at your head. You goin' ter tell me what you know about me and the killin'. You goin' ter tell me who told *you* about these things. And then I'm goin' ter shoot you. Now, you ready?'

'If you're going to shoot me anyway, you might as well do it now, Spider,' said David defiantly, 'because I'm not going to tell you anything.'

'Waal, now,' said Spider sarcastically, 'ef we ain't a little hero! I sure *am* goin' ter shoot you, but I'm goin' ter make you talk first. There's ways, you know,' continued the desperado, with an evil leer, 'there's ways! Like the Chinese torture, fer instance. I could feed you cold sago pudden, six times a day. Thet's one way. Then agin, I could put cactus spikes in the feet of your socks an' fire a few bullets round your toes ter make you dance. Jest think thet over afore you tell me you won't talk!'

And he would do it too, thought David. Clearly the man was villain enough for anything. But then into David's mind there came the words of Lofty Cassidy, right at the beginning of the adventure that had now brought him to this fateful spot . . . 'The rules bein' that once you get started on the adventure you won't never give in nor turn back but see it right through to the end. *Even if it means being shot or drowned.*' And David and Toby had given their promise to Uncle Septimus that they *would* see the thing through. So David gritted his teeth and said: 'You can shoot me— but I tell you nothing, Spider.'

Spider rubbed his horny hands together. 'Waal, then,' he said, 'if Chinese torture an' cactuses in your socks don't frighten you, then I've got a whole lot worse tortures. Like the Mongolian torture, where I pulls the hairs out of your head—one at a time. You got plenty of hair, I see. And there's . . . well, there's dozens of other tortures I knows and each is worse than the one before. So you kin set and think what's a-goin' to happen to you whiles I lights up my pipe and makes up my mind which torture to use.' And Spider fumbled in his pocket and brought out his pipe.

The end was coming now and it seemed impossible for David to escape his doom. But as that word 'impossible' floated through his mind, he suddenly seemed to hear, far away and faint, the lilt of an Irish jig played on the violin and a voice that said: 'Impossible! Why, me bhoyos, I admit no such word in my philosophery ... Remember the inspirin' history av Paddy McGinty's goat ...

> *He could chew up any ropes—he could bite through any chains,*
> *For McGinty's was a goat that knew just how ot use his brains.*
> *When they locked him in the prison, swearin' he'd escape no more*
> *Why, he simply put his head to work ... and butted down the door.'*

David tried to 'put his head to work', as the song said. He thought and he thought and he thought, but no idea seemed to come. He heard Spider utter a low curse because his pipe had gone out. Then there was the scrape of a match and the flame lit up the bowl and long stem of the desperado's pipe. And suddenly, out of David's hard thinking, there came an idea.

Throwing one leg out, he kicked his toe hard into the earth, sending a shower of sand and pebbles right into Spider's face. The pipe flew from the man's mouth and shattered its stem against a rock. With a horrible oath, Spider leaned forward and jabbed his pistol into David's chest.

Then, with a great effort, he mastered the murderous impulse. 'Very clever! Very clever!' he said with a twisted grin. 'You wanted to trick me into shootin' you so's you could escape the torture and answerin' my questions. Jes' you wait 'til I finish me smoke!' And Spider picked up the pieces of his pipe and looked at it ruefully.

'Now what kin I do ter mend thet broken stem?' he said, and felt in his pockets. 'Why, now,' he said suddenly, 'ef you ain't saved my life, youngster. Here's thet little tube o' wood I took off'n you. Now ef I fits one end in here ... and the other end in there ... why, there's me pipe almost as good as new!' He looked at his handiwork admiringly.

So far so good. Spider had done just what David hoped he would do, and repaired his pipe with the bamboo tube that could be used to send a message to Uncle Septimus.

The whole question now was this: was the holder of the tube supposed to *blow* through it or *suck* through it? All that could be learned from David's trick on Spider was whether the tube would work when it was sucked through.

Anxiously he watched the desperado as Spider began to draw on his pipe. David strained his eyes looking among the rocks. He stared up into the sky. He strained his ears for the slightest sound that would indicate that the bamboo tube had sent out its call. But he could see nothing and hear nothing. His plan had failed: for all Spider's drawing on the pipe, nothing was happening.

And now Spider was sucking even harder on the pipe. And David saw that he seemed unable to get any smoke through it.

'Gosh durn it!' cried the cowboy, 'ef some o' thet gravel you kicked up at me ain't blocked the stem of my pipe!' And the desperado took a deep breath and *blew* through it to clear the obstruction.

And it was at that moment that David saw it . . . a black shadow, like a bird with huge wings, that blocked out the light of the moon for just an instant, then descended, slowly and silently as falling thistledown, and came to rest behind the bandit.

David bit his lip so as not to cry out as he looked at the messenger of Uncle Septimus. Its head towered over Spider, who sat again enjoying his pipe and chuckling at the torture he was about to inflict. The head of the newcomer resembled that of a wolf, with sharp up-pointed ears. Its eyes shone with an eerie amber light and it bared a mouthful of huge white fangs. As David watched, the vast black creature silently raised its huge wings above its head and David saw they were rimmed with gleaming steel talons. It could be nothing else than a giant bat—but one bigger and more terrible than any other creature that roamed the skies.

And suddenly Spider spoke.

'You look worried, tenderfoot,' he mocked, 'and well you might, 'kase I've jest decided to start on the first torture I'm goin' ter give you.' He rose to his feet . . . and at that moment the enormous black wings descended and folded across the desperado, pinning his arms to his side.

Spider tried to struggle. He flung his head back to see what it was that was gripping him. His eyes fell on the baleful eyes and dripping fangs of the monster and, with a scream of mortal terror, he fainted.

And now the Giant Bat spoke. (There's a bit of a problem here, because as you may know, the noises that bats make can't be heard by human ears, and although this was an extra big bat, it was probably shouting its loudest so that David could make out what it said. Even so we'll have to use very small type to give you some idea of how tiny its voice seemed to David.)

The Bat said, 'Have you a message for Chief Cobwebb?'

'Yes,' said David, feeling in his pockets, 'will you please take this badge to Uncle Septimus and show him how it has been folded to make the Big O brand look like the Double C of Cobwebb Cowboys.'

'Thank you,' said the Bat, hooking the piece of cloth on a shining steel claw. 'Is that all?'

'Oh no,' said David. 'Will you please take this man Spider as well. Because he killed Paddy Murphy's partner and tried to get Paddy hanged for it. And he can also tell Uncle Septimus all about the plans of Sheriff Jabez Gunn and his Big O gangsters for driving the Moccasin Indians off their land.'

The Giant Bat drew itself up even taller. 'Here, wait a minute,' it said. 'I can't take him! Messengers aren't allowed to carry anything except mails.'

'Well, he's a male, isn't he?' said David quickly.

The Bat thought a moment. 'Why, yes,' it replied, 'I suppose you're right. Yes, indeed. Well, that's settled then. No time for gossip. Don't worry, Sir, the male will get through.' And silently the Bat soared into the air with its limp burden and vanished in the blackness of the night.

David was alone—and between him and the end of Paddy Murphy's tunnel there were two armed desperadoes on the look-out for the return of their evil companion.

CHAPTER 21

PRINCE RAM JAMWHAM FOOLS A SHERIFF

TOBY, trapped under the enormous circus tent, had to make a quick decision. If he ducked back down the hole he would have to tunnel a way out from under the canvas—and he wasn't at all sure how to set about that. On the other hand, if he crawled under the canvas to the edge of the tent, he might be seen by the circus workers who were awaiting the order to hoist the Big Top. He decided that he must take the risk of being seen and he set off, keeping as close to the ground as possible, to wriggle his way out.

Luck was on his side, because as he got to the edge of the tent and peeped out, there was a shout from the other side of the tent and a great scurry of feet as all the workers on his side ran over to help haul up the great centre-pole. In a flash Toby was out in the open. He dived beneath a group of covered living-wagons and crawled beneath them to the edge of the trail that led to Gopher City.

The sun was now well above the horizon and Toby sauntered along the trail, watching the activity round the circus tent. The great roof had now been hauled up the centre-pole and men were pulling on ropes and hammering away at tent pegs. A very strange-looking crowd they were, too. Every man he could see was wearing a long, white, wide-sleeved gown that fell right to his ankles, and each had a headdress made from a large square of white cloth that fell down over the back of the neck and was held in place by a circlet of silken cords. All the men had thin black moustaches and small pointed black beards and they looked very strange and very fierce indeed.

Toby was beginning to wonder if he'd really found his way to Gopher City or whether some strange magic had brought him to another country, when he saw the huge notice over the entrance to the tent.

MUSTAPHA KAMIL'S

GREAT ARABIAN CIRCUS!!

The Sensation of the Orient!

A placard on the ground announced that the circus was in Gopher City for *One Day Only . . . Admission 20 Cents . . . Hitching Posts and Free Fodder for All Horses*. That offer was a pretty good idea, Toby thought. In a place like Gopher City, where almost everybody went about on horseback, it really ought to draw the crowds.

He wondered, however, if the fierce-looking Arabs could do anything on horsebacks or with guns that the hard-riding cowboys of the area could not do—and what would happen if the cowboys felt that they hadn't got their 20-cents' worth? But the wily Mustapha Kamil seemed to have thought of that, for there was a notice outside the ticket office:

All Shooting Irons and Ammunition to be Checked in here before Entry

The rumble of galloping hooves behind him made Toby swing round. Coming down the trail at breakneck pace, a huge black stallion was being urged on with wild yells by one of the circus Arabs, his white gown billowing out behind him. Toby turned to watch the horseman pass. But, just as his frothing steed drew abreast of Toby, the Arab leaped from the saddle, thrust a piece of paper into Toby's hand, shot forward

86

in a double somersault and then, with a final incredible leap, landed again in the saddle and galloped off in a cloud of dust towards the Main Street of Gopher City.

Toby looked at the paper. It was a handbill describing the circus attractions, and Toby began to wish he had 20 cents in his pocket and could go to the performance instead of having the dangerous job of questioning One-Eye Joe. The handbill, as you can see on the next page, promised all sorts of thrills.

Toby walked into the Main Street of Gopher City and when he saw it he felt even more strongly that he'd much rather be going to the circus. The Main Street was, in fact, about the only street that Gopher City had. There were just two rows of wooden buildings, set pretty wide apart on a wide patch of sand that had been churned up by the hooves of thousands of horses and cattle. The only building that really looked any different from the others was the Gopher City Saloon. Already there were numbers of horses fastened to the hitching rail outside the saloon and through its open doors came the sound of a piano and raucous singing. Toby guessed that the wild cowboys of the Big O outfit were already in town to see the circus and had begun to make a day of it.

Toby found One-Eye Joe's little shop and went in. The shoemaker was bent over his last and, without looking up, he called, 'Whaddya want?'

Toby took a deep breath and said, 'Please, I've been sent to collect some boots you're mending for . . . for . . .' and he hesitated as though he had forgotten the name.

The shoemaker lifted his head and snapped, 'Well, whose boots are they, boy?'

'I'm sorry,' said Toby, 'but I'm a new boy working for the Big O. The man's name has gone clean out of my head . . . but I can describe him. He's the one who's right leg is shorter than his left.'

'Oh, you mean Spider,' answered the man. And then he looked straight at Toby with his one eye, which was very blue and steely. 'Funny you could fergit a simple

MUSTAPHA KAMIL'S

GREAT

ORIENTAL CIRCUS

——SEE——

THE DESERT RIDERS!!!
Daring Deeds
On Milk-white Steeds!

❧❧

THE 12 DAUNTLESS DERVISHES!!!
They walk on fire—
And don't perspire.

❧❧

— ALSO —

ABDUL THE DAMNED
Here's the mule no man can ride—
A dollar each for all who've tried.

❧❧

— SPECIAL FOR THE CHILDREN —

Rides on TINY, the World's Smallest Elephant
(direct from India with his trainer, Prince Ram
Jamwham)

Also BIMBO, the Juggling Clown, and

ALL THE FUN OF THE FAIR!!!!

name like that, boy,' he said, 'and Spider's memory seems as bad as yours. Why, he done told me himself that Sheriff Gunn would take his boots down to the ranch fer him. I handed 'em into Gunn's office not twenty minnits ago. Spider must want 'em in a hurry. Look here, youngster, you jes' look after the shop fer me and I'll go 'cross the road an' get 'em fer you.'

He sidled out of the shop with a shifty smile that made Toby suspicious, so he stood by the window and watched One-Eye Joe as he went into Jabez Gunn's office. After a moment another man came out and went to the saloon. When he came out again, there were five or six others with him. Toby noticed that all of them wore the sign of the Big O on their shirts.

And that made him think of his own shirt, and he looked down. Although it was very dirty, because of his underground journey, the brand mark of the Double C was quite clear. One-Eye Joe had recognised him for a spy and had gone for help. The men across the road were coming to get him!

With one bound Toby was out of the shop and pelting back up Main Street as fast as he could go. The street was now crowded with people and Toby dodged among them with only one thought in his mind: to get to the circus and hide among the wagons while his pursuers streamed past to hunt for him among the tumbled rocks of the nearby hillside.

Already he could hear a great hubbub behind, lots of shouting and then, more menacing still, the drumming of hooves. He was out of the street now and nearing the circus wagons when, thundering down the trail towards him, came a stage coach. It swept past him, the hooves of its team of six horses stirring up a cloud of dust that for a time blotted out all sight of Toby from his pursuers. With a sob of relief he made for hiding under the circus wagons.

And then, suddenly, there was the swirl of a white gown, a vision of a fierce Arab face, and two strong arms seized Toby and heaved him over the tailboard into one of the wagons. Thrusting him into a chair, the

89

Arab put his face close to Toby's, pressed a finger to his lips and said, 'Sssh!' Then, rummaging in a big box, he drew out an Arab headdress and long white gown, held it out to Toby, and pointed to himself with a smile. As Toby put on the disguise the Arab pointed to his moustache and then, with a sort of black crayon, he gave Toby a really fierce moustache.

By now the pursuers had fanned out to look for their prey and some of them were coming among the circus people, asking if they had seen a young cowboy.

The Arab took Toby's arm and pointed towards the circus tent where the fierce little Indian, Prince Ram Jamwham, was preparing Tiny, the elephant, for the circus procession. The Arab gave a shrill whistle and the Prince turned, then beckoned imperiously to Toby.

There was nothing for it but to go . . . at any rate, thought Toby, whatever they want to do with me, they don't mean to give me up to Jabez Gunn.

When Toby reached the Prince, Tiny, the elephant —in its heavy trappings of diamond-studded blue silk that covered everything except its eyes and white-painted trunk—was kneeling in readiness for its passengers. It looked a frail little thing under the great howdah and the tall golden umbrella that were strapped on its back.

Prince Ram Jamwham, whose turban seemed nearly as big as himself, climbed into his seat and with a snap of his fingers, signed Toby to the seat beside him. Then, at a sharp word of command, Tiny rose to its feet and ambled towards the group of questioning cowboys.

Toby's pursuers were having no luck with the Arabs, who answered all their questions with a flood of strange words that the cowboys couldn't understand. When Tiny ambled up, Sheriff Gunn wheeled his horse round and shouted, 'Hey, you! Do you speak English?'

In his high-pitched voice the little Prince replied, 'Yes, please. I speak English. Also understand, isn't it?'

'Well, we're a-huntin' a criminal,' growled the Sheriff. 'He jes' done robbed a store while the owner

*The fierce Prince Ram Jamwham, from India, and his
mysterious passenger, seated in the howdah on Tiny, the
World's Smallest Elephant.*

was out.' And he went on to give a description of Toby. 'You seen anyone like that?' he ended.

'Why, yess. I see boy exactly like so,' answered the Prince.

'Hear that!' cried the Sheriff to the others. 'We're on his trail! Well, which way did he go?' he snapped at Prince Ram Jamwham.

'That way,' said the Prince, pointing towards Gopher City.

'Don't lie to me!' Sheriff Gunn's hand closed on his revolver. 'He was seen headin' this way—how could he turn back without runnin' right into us?'

'So sorry,' answered the Prince, 'but matter is one of extremist simplicity, yes. You see, this very smart young person jump on back axle of stage-coach . . .'

The Sheriff let out a roar of anger. 'Golldarn it!' he cried. 'He rode right through the middle of us, hidden in a cloud o' dust. The stage coach'll be ten miles the other side o' Gopher City by now. After it, lads!' And off, on the wrong trail, roared Toby's pursuers.

Truly these circus people had saved his life! Toby turned to Prince Ram Jamwham. 'Prince,' he began, 'I just don't know how to thank you . . .'

But before he could say any more, the Prince burst into a huge bellow of laughter. He thrust a great hand out towards Toby and answered, in a very different kind of voice this time, 'Why, boy Toby! I believe you sure don't reckernise us. Hev you forgotten your old pardners, Lofty Cassidy an' that world-renowned elephoss, Fanty?'

And as Lofty pumped Toby's arm up and down, Fanty raised his trunk high in the air and trumpeted a peal of pure delight.

CHAPTER 22

DOUBLE AMBUSH

THE task that faced David, when the Giant Bat had flown off with Spider, was how to get back down the trail and pass the cowboys' campfire without being seen. Once he had done that, he felt it would be easy to make his way up the hillside to the cave in safety because, if they were watching at all, they would be looking in the other direction for Spider's return.

So he kept in the shadows at the side of the trail and worked his way along from rock to rock. It was not long before he saw the glow of the campfire and then he moved very slowly and carefully indeed until he could look into the little hollow. But there were no cowboys there. None of their gear remained and the fire had sunk to a glowing patch of embers.

It was obvious to David that the men had gone off without waiting for their companion, Spider. So he stepped out into the middle of the trail and set off at a smart pace.

As he did so, a hard voice barked from behind him, 'Stick 'em up, boy, an' stay right thar!'

Cold fear clutched at David's heart as he realised that he had walked into a trap. He swung round, hands held high, and the look of dismay on his face brought shouts of laughter from the two villains of the Big O outfit who lounged, one at each side of the trail, with revolvers at the ready.

'You sure are a tenderfoot,' gasped one, 'ter walk through enemy territory without ever lookin' over your shoulder ter see if you're bein' stalked!'

'We been followin' you fer the last ten minutes,' said the other. 'Now, quit the jokin'. Where's Spider?'

Well, this was really a problem. David felt that if he said, 'Oh, a Giant Bat swooped down and carried him off into the sky,' the two desperadoes would be quite likely to shoot him on the spot. So he said nothing. And this made his captors very suspicious.

'There's only one way you could git away from Spider—an' that's by shootin' him,' said one of the men. He turned to the other. 'Guess we'd better take him back up the trail with us an' look fer Spider's body.'

'Ain't no sense in that,' was the reply. 'Ef that boy's here, then Spider's been shot. Ef Spider's been shot, then thet boy shot him. Ain't no time fer huntin' a dead man—we got to be back at the ranch ready for the big raid on the Moccasins . . .'

David pricked up his ears at this news, but his blood ran cold when the cowboy continued, '. . . So I say "shoot the boy" an' let's get on our way.'

'O.K.,' growled the other, and very deliberately he began to raise his revolver. And . . .

At that moment a number of things happened all at once. The ground beneath the feet of the two desperadoes seemed to open. They screamed with terror and their revolvers went flying across the rocks as they sank rapidly down, down, down, into the earth until only their heads, wide-open shouting mouths and staring eyes could be seen above the sand and stones of the trail.

Then, between the trapped desperadoes, the earth seemed to boil and up came two long, hairy arms and two hands with long, sharp talons. The hands descended on the heads of the cowboys, crushing their hats down firmly over their eyes, and, with a great heave, Mr Patrick Murphy, the human mole, levered himself out of his latest tunnel and clasped David by the hand.

'Better late than never, David me bhoyo,' he said. 'I'd been seekin' all round for you when I saw these two ruffians settin' up their ambush. Will you tell me now what's happening?'

So David told him the whole story about Spider and how the other two cowboys had revealed that the big attack on the Indians was planned to take place very soon.

'Well, those two won't be takin' part in any raid!' chuckled Mr Murphy, 'and I expect your Uncle Septimus will soon be on the way to help the Moccasins. But I'm worried about your brother.' And he told David about sending Toby to One-Eye Joe. 'You see,' he said, 'if One-Eye knew that Spider was out here, then he'd know he had his boots with him and that'd make him suspicious of Toby straight away. So we'd better be on our way to Gopher City as fast as we can.'

They clambered up to the cave and dived into the tunnel, and with Mr Murphy chatting away to him as they crawled along, it seemed quite a short time to David before they arrived in Paddy's headquarters, where a great bowl of Puffery-leaf soup was already bubbling away on the stove. Like Toby, David was puzzled by the notice about the Trolls and he questioned Mr Murphy closely about the course of the Wailing River.

'Where it ends I can't say,' Paddy told him. 'But I do know that it rises somewhere beneath these hills. Then it flows out across the plain and into more hills. There it goes under the mountains that rise awful high into what folks call the Mist Curtain. I guess that's about all I know. And now it's time to be on our way.'

It was a long crawl, but at last the tunnel began to slope upwards and finally Mr Murphy and David poked their heads above ground.

'Why, here's a mysterious thing,' cried Paddy, in a worried voice. ' 'Tis terrible dark and yet me mind tells me that 'tis only early evening. Where's the sun?'

And then he gasped as, out of the darkness, a deep voice called, 'D'you want some sunshine, Paddy? Well —here it is!!'

And suddenly all around them was floodlit by the huge arc-lamps of the circus.

'Oh, heavens preserve us!' shrieked Mr Murphy. ' 'Tis surrounded I am by a thousand wild Ayrabs and an ephelant. Oh dear, I'm goin' mad . . . at long last the weight av me intellect has broken me poor brain.'

And then, there was Toby in front of them, seizing the hands of both and crying, 'Come up, come up! It's all right! They aren't Arabs . . . they're cowboys from the Double C outfit and they've been putting on a circus show. You've come up in the middle of the ring!'

And now the cowboys were all round Paddy, clapping him on the back making him welcome, while amid the uproar, Toby was trying to explain to David all that had happened to him and David was telling him about *his* adventures.

CHAPTER 23

PADDY MURPHY IN HOT WATER

SUDDENLY, in the middle of the uproar, the deep sound of a bronze bell throbbed through the circus tent and at once silence fell. And now they heard a voice, not loud, but very clear—a voice that seemed full of laughter.

'Gentlemen,' said the voice, 'this is Captain Cobwebb. On behalf of Cobwebb's Cowboys, I welcome our young adventurers, David and Toby, and with them, their friend and helper, Mr Patrick Aloysius Demosthenes Ignatius Murphy, whose name has now been cleared by the confession of the evil Spider. Please be seated, gentlemen, and listen closely. I am about to make an important announcement.'

The voice of Captain Cobwebb seemed to come from a large armchair that had been placed in the circus ring, and the cowboys of the Double C, in their Arab disguises, took their places in a great half-moon in front of the chair.

Poor Mr Murphy became even more bemused when David and Toby tried to tell him that Uncle

Septimus was really sitting there and speaking to them, only he was invisible because he'd lived so long among such people as fairies and so forth. Then Prince Ram Jamwham came up in his huge turban and said his name was Lofty Cassidy, and after that a tall thin clown with a great red nose and a tall pointed hat thrust out a large hand and said, 'Remember me? I'm Cowboy Lefty.'

All this was too much for Paddy. He swayed from side to side and scratched away at his head. 'Arrah, now,' he moaned. 'Try as I might to stimulerate me intellect, there's not a thing that will come of it. It's going crazy I must be, what with findin' Gopher City full of Ayrabs an' ephelants an' talkin' chairs! Stay beside me, me bhoyos, an' pray that I returns to sanctity.' So David and Toby linked arms with him to console him and waited to hear what Uncle Septimus had to say.

'When the man Spider confessed that he was the killer of Mr Murphy's partner,' said Uncle Septimus, 'he also told us that a great raid was to be made this very night on our friends, the Moccasins. That evil Sheriff, Jabez Gunn, intends to throw his whole force of armed desperadoes against the Moccasins and drive them from their territory for ever. He wants to take over the legendary hill of gold that they have guarded for generations. But we have told the Moccasins about these plans, and about the trick of making the brand of the Big O outfit look like the Double C of Cobwebb's cowboys. It is thanks to the fine detective work—and the courage—of David and Toby here, and their friend, Mr Murphy, that this treachery has been exposed . . .'

There was a cheer from the cowboys of the Double C and then the voice of Captain Cobwebb continued: 'But I see our young friends are looking somewhat baffled. Have they any questions?'

Toby and David looked at each other and then David said timidly, 'Well, yes, we have a question, we can't understand about the circus. I mean, why put on a circus show for these g-g-gangsters from the Big O?'

'The reason,' answered Uncle Septimus with a chuckle, 'is that we wanted to have the Big O outfit all together in one place where we could keep an eye on them while we did certain things—things that will enable us to round up the whole gang without, we hope, a shot being fired. A circus was the one thing that would really bring them all together and once they were all inside the circus tent, we could get on with our preparations without them knowing what we were doing.'

'But what *did* you do, Uncle Septimus?' asked Toby. 'I didn't notice anything.'

There was a roar of laughter from the cowboys.

'If *you* didn't notice, then we must have been pretty clever,' said Uncle Septimus, 'because you are a very noticing kind of boy. But have patience, you will know the answer very soon. In half an hour we strike tent and the circus moves out of Gopher City. By the time it is dark, every man of Cobwebb's Cowboys must be in position at the Indian camp ready for the attack.

'This means,' added Uncle Septimus, 'that David and Toby, who already wear the badge of the Double C outfit, will naturally be with us. But I am sorry to say that Mr Murphy cannot join us, because he is not a member of our band.'

Lefty sprang to his feet. 'I move we elect Paddy Murphy a full member of Cobwebb's Cowboys for the help he's given in finding out the truth about the raids on the Moccasins,' he said.

A great roar of applause went up from the cowboys and Uncle Septimus said, 'Well, it seems that we are all agreed . . .'

But at that moment Lofty Cassidy stamped forward to the centre of the circle and, with a great wink to his friends, cried out. 'Objection!'

'State your objection to the candidate!' said Captain Cobwebb.

'Waal,' drawled Lofty, 'if he rides with us into the Moccasin camp—all covered with hair like he is—the

Injuns will be terrified. They'll think the Ugudugu-
djuk has come to eat 'em up. I don't object ter Paddy
Murphy, Captain, but I does object to all thet hair.'

'Objection sustained,' said Captain Cobwebb gravely,
but there was a chuckle in the voice from the chair.
'Hear then, Patrick Aloysius Demosthenes Ignatius . . .'

'Oh, please, yer Honour,' broke in Paddy pleadingly,
'not all them names again. Me initials is P.A.D.I.,
which spells Paddy, or near enough.'

'Very well, Paddy it shall be,' answered Captain Cobwebb. 'Hear then, Paddy Murphy! You are elected to
the noble band of cowboys of the Double C Ranch. But
this is subject to the condition that this, er, unacceptable
hair is removed . . .'

'But arrah, now, yer Honour,' cried Paddy in distress,
' 'tis not in nature . . . I can't *un*grow me hair, now,
can I?'

There was a great shout from the cowboys and a
babble of laughing voices.

'Don't worry, Paddy, we'll get it off for you!'

'Where's the hoss-clippers?'

'No, singe it off with a blow-lamp!'

'Lather him all over.'

'Yes, that's it . . . Bring your razors, boys!'

The cowboys seized on the joke, and as they rushed
at him poor Paddy gave one terrified yell and dived
for the floor, scrabbling away with his great claws to
get back into his tunnel. But he could not escape his
fate. Before his head was half-way into the earth, Fanty
the elephorse had wrapped his trunk round Paddy's
middle and lifted him, kicking and struggling, high
into the air while the cheering cowboys manhandled a
horse-trough full of soapy hot water to the middle of
the ring, and stood around waving an assortment of
instruments that ranged from horse-clippers to bowie
knives and great old-fashioned razors.

'All right now, Fanty,' called Lofty Cassidy. 'Drop
him!' And with a wild, despairing yell that was cut
short by a watery gurgle and a cloud of bubbles, Mr

Patrick Aloysius Demosthenes Ignatius Murphy vanished into a swiftly rising mountain of lather.

It was a long time before the operation was finished but at last a pink-faced Mr Murphy stood before a mirror his new cowboy outfit hidden beneath a white Arab robe. He looked at his reflection and seemed very pleased with it.

'Sure, me bhoyos,' he said to David and Toby, 'the Murphys were always a handsome lot an' the world will be a more joyous place now that I've been dehairified, painful though 'twas. Besides which, I feel pounds lighter—though not so warm as I did before. I could do with a good gallop on a hoss to restore me circumlocation.'

The great gong boomed again. And in the silence that followed, the voice of Captain Cobwebb announced, 'Strike the tent at once, boys, and take to the trail! We are on our way to the final showdown with Jabez Gunn and his villainous followers.'

CHAPTER 24

THE NIGHT OF THE SNORING HORSES

VERY quickly the circus tent was pulled down and stowed, and the wagon train moved off with the cowboys, muffled in their Arab robes, riding at each side. David, Toby and Paddy Murphy kept together as the procession made its way down Main Street. A few loungers shouted a goodnight as they passed, then turned into the noisy saloon to tell their friends that the circus people were on their way out.

The evil Jabez Gunn, sitting at a table with his lieutenant, was pleased at the news. 'The circus folk told me that they're playing tomorrow at the Double C Ranch,' he said to his companion. 'That means no

Double C cowboys will be stirring away from the ranch before tomorrow night. We chose the right night fer the big attack. Jes' wait till the circus has turned up the fork in the trail. Then we ride in. No witnesses to see what we do. Shoot down the Moccasin braves and drive the rest away. They'll spread the story that it was the Double C . . . so be sure, Jake, that every man wears his false badge and a mask.'

'I done told 'em already,' said the man called Jake. 'Spider and the other two ain't turned up yet, though. I hope there's nawthin' wrong.'

Jabez Gunn tossed back a glass of raw spirit and laughed harshly. 'Don't worry about Spider,' he said 'He'll be along—Spider wouldn't miss a killing.'

Meanwhile, miles down the trail to the Moccasin camp, the circus train jogged along until, on a stony ridge, the fork in the road was reached. Here Lofty Cassidy called a halt. The cowboys tore off their Arab disguises and tossed them into the wagons.

'An' a great an' lastin' pleasure will it be to get rid of that Ayrab outfit,' declared Paddy Murphy. 'Fer a man at my age an' rotunderosity, 'tis embrassagin' ter be ridin' around in a white nightie.'

Then, as the wagons took off over the hill, Lofty called his men together.

'These are Captain Cobwebb's orders,' he said. 'We ride down to the Moccasin camp. Well outside the camp, we space ourselves out, find whatever cover we can, and lie down and wait. As soon as we hear Jabez Gunn and his men coming, I'll give the Moccasins a signal. From then on the Indians know exactly what's going to happen. *We* don't move in until I say so. Today *we* gave a circus show fer Jabez Gunn and his gangsters : tonight, boys, we're goin' ter watch *them* give one !'

When they came to the place for the ambush, David and Toby found a little ridge of boulders and settled down with Paddy Murphy for the long vigil. Peering out they could see below them the black shapes of the tall wigwams. In the centre of the encampment the huge Totem pole was lit by the flames of the camp fire. Not a soul was in sight. Anyone riding into the camp would think that the Indians were all sound asleep.

The hours passed slowly. The flames of the camp fire began to sink lower. Lofty Cassidy, making a tour of his forces, crawled over to them. 'All well?' he asked, and was just moving away when Paddy Murphy stifled a sneeze and hissed: 'Stop a minnit, me behoyo. I can feel the spalpeens a-coming.'

'*Feel* them?' whispered Lofty. 'What d'you mean, feel them?'

'Sure, I drove me bowie-knife into the earth,' replied Paddy, 'and then I bit on the handle.'

'But how does that tell you anything, Paddy?' said David.

'Why now,' declared Paddy, ' 'tis the hooves of the hosses that shakes the earth and the vibrifications is picked up by me knife. Now, I have a loose tooth in front and when I bites on the knife, them same vibrifications shakes me loose tooth. When it shakes, it tickles me gums. And when me gums tickle, I sneezes. Well, you heard me, didn't you?'

But before Lofty could reply, David, who has a very keen sense of hearing, held up a hand.

'Ssh!' he said. 'Paddy's right. I can hear them.'

They all listened very hard and finally Lofty said, 'I hear it now. They'll soon be here. Now I'll warn the Moccasins.' He cupped his hands round his mouth and suddenly the mournful cry of a hunting owl echoed across the hillside.

Almost immediately Indian braves began to come out of the wigwams. The drumming of hooves grew louder and louder. The Indians appeared not to hear anything. They formed into groups and collected round the camp fire. Now the very earth was shaking to the mad gallop of the desperadoes. And then, suddenly, with a wild fusillade of revolver shots, the masked bandits burst into the Moccasin encampment.

'The tall one in the lead,' whispered Lofty, 'that's Jabez Gunn.'

In an ever-tightening circle Gunn led his screeching horde round and round the Indian braves, squeezing them closer and closer to the camp fire.

Then suddenly, Gunn wrenched his great black stallion to a standstill and, as the circle of bandits came to a halt, he cried, 'Shoot 'em down, boys! Shoot 'em down!'

David and Toby leaped to their feet. 'But we can't let them do this!' cried Toby, and the boys were darting forward when Lofty's long arms reached out and pulled them down beside him.

'Watch, watch!' he said. 'Look at the Indians . . .'

The boys looked—and gasped. Below, the maddened desperadoes were pouring bullets into the close-packed Indian crowd. Great clouds of gunsmoke, glowing blood-red in the light of the camp fire, rolled around them.

But . . . *not one single Indian was falling down.*

While Jabez Gunn screamed, 'Shoot! Shoot!' the Moccasins simply walked or stood right under the muzzles of the bandits' guns. The shooting began to waver, then die away. The bandits sat on their horses transfixed, then began to edge their mounts back, away from the Indians.

'I can't understand it,' muttered David.

'Thank your Uncle Septimus for this,' laughed Lofty. 'Toby, surely you remember that at the circus all the audience had to hand in their guns and ammunition belts before they could come in? Well, while they were inside enjoying themselves, we took all their bullets away and replaced 'em with blanks! But look . . . now . . . look!'

For down in the camp an even stranger thing was happening . . . something that has never happened before. Hundreds and hundreds of books have been written about Red Indians, but in not one of them does the writer ever say that he's seen an Indian laugh. A smile, maybe—once every fifty years or so—but a laugh, never. But now, under the useless guns of the would-be killers, history was being made. Great bellows of

103

laughter came from the 'victims' of Jabez Gunn's attack. Indian braves put their hands across their eyes and wept tears of mirth. They howled with glee. They staggered about, their knees weak with laughter. They slapped each other on the back, they pointed shaking fingers at the desperadoes and hooted and screeched with mirth.

It was the black-hearted Jabez Gunn who recovered himself first.

'We've been tricked!' he roared. 'Ride your hosses at 'em, boys! Trample 'em down under the hosses!'

His cry rallied the desperadoes. Cursing and shouting, they dug their spurs into the flanks of their mounts and urged them viciously towards the helpless Moccasins.

'Oh, the evil brutes!' cried Toby.

But . . . what was this? The horses did not move forward at all—not one of them. Instead they began to sway from side to side. They sank down on their haunches. Their front legs folded. And—as their terrified riders struggled to get clear—they all rolled over on their sides. And if anybody ever tells you that horses don't snore—don't believe him. These horses snored in a hundred different keys and they snored so loudly that they drowned the bandits' cries of dismay and the Indian yells of laughter.

'Is this another of the tricks you played during the circus show?' giggled David, as the great waves of horse snores echoed around the hillside.

'Y-yes,' gasped Lofty, 'we had a notice saying that people could leave their hosses outside the tent and we would give 'em a feed during the performance. Your Uncle Septimus had a special sleeping powder made up to put in their nosebags.'

But now he leaped to his feet and gave a shrill whistle, which was repeated from man to man of the Double C. 'This is where we move in,' he cried. 'Come on! The Moccasins aren't in a fit state to round up them villains. We'll have to do that.'

And he was right. For the Indian braves were by now so helpless with laughter that they were rolling

104

The evil Jabez Gunn fires his six-shooter at an Indian at point-blank range and all his victim does is to laugh uproariously and jig about in the Moccasin Joy Dance. Nothing disconcerts a desperado more than this kind of thing.

about on the ground, waving their arms and kicking their legs in the air.

But as the baffled desperadoes tried to slink off to safety, they found their way blocked on every side by the cowboys of the Double C who advanced upon them.

'Rope 'em all together, boys!' called Lofty.. 'All— except Jabez Gunn.' Then he cried loudly, 'The game's up, Gunn! You're licked an' there's nothin' you kin do about it. Step forward, Jabez, you dog. I'm a-goin' to rope you up myself.'

But from behind the black mask of Jabez Gunn, there came the snarled response: 'That's *what you* think, cowboy!'

CHAPTER 25

JABEZ GUNN PLAYS HIS ACE

EVERYBODY thought that the words of Jabez Gunn were an empty boast. What could he do, after all? The cowboys continued to tie up their prisoners, helped by the laughing Indian braves, among whom David and Toby noticed the slim figure of Little Cloud. In the shadows among the tents stood the old Chief, Bald Eagle, with the elders of the tribe, and already the squaws and the children were tumbling from the wigwams to see the rounding up of the desperadoes of the Big O.

Lofty hitched up his belt, and with his right hand resting on the butt of his revolver, continued to advance towards Jabez Gunn.

'Yeah,' he said, 'thet's exactly what I *do* think, Mr Gunn. I'm a-goin' to rope you up. An' if you try any funny business, Gunn, I'll shoot you through the leg . . . bekase I'm goin' ter take you alive, Jabez, and hand you over ter face a judge an' jury.'

'You fool!' hissed Gunn. 'Take one more step towards me and I'll blow meself and every manjack

106

among you sky-high. Look at that . . .' and he flung up his arm, ' . . . see what I've got in me hand? That's a parcel o' dynamite. Ef you want ter see tomorrow, jest give way an' let me pass quietly now. An' let nobody ride after me, or I'll blow the road up in front of him.'

There was a stir among the prisoners and Jake, the evil lieutenant of the desperado, called out, 'Well done, Jabez! Now tell 'em to untie us an' we'll all go together.'

Jabez Gunn turned his head with a sneer. 'What!' he snarled, 'take you scurvy, useless rats along wi' me? Never. You can rot in jail, fer all I care. Now out o' my way, Cassidy!'

There was nothing that Lofty could do—nothing, it seemed, that anyone could do. If innocent people were not to die, the killer must be allowed to go. With the pleas of his former companions ringing in his ears, Jabez Gunn swaggered through the firelit camp towards the darkness outside—and freedom.

Everybody—Moccasins, cowboys, and the companions he had deserted, watched him in silence. But no one had yet seen the full depths of Gunn's vileness. For, as he reached the edge of the camp, he turned.

'Well, so long folks,' he jeered. 'Thanks fer the entertainment. An' now it's my turn to stand treat. After all, it's the last time I'll be seein' you. Hev this on me . . .'

And with a shout of evil laughter he flung the packet of dynamite high into the air—towards the very centre of the camp, the great Totem pole and the leaping flames of the camp fire! And as all eyes turned in horror to the falling high explosive, Jabez Gunn vanished into the darkness.

'On your faces, everybody!' yelled Lofty Cassidy and the whole throng of people flung themselves to the ground. Down . . . down . . . down . . . came the parcel of dynamite. It was falling towards the Totem pole . . . nearer . . . nearer . . . and then it vanished into one of the great grinning mouths of the figures on the Totem.

A moment later a shattering explosion shook the camp. Dust and rock fragments spewed from the mouths of the Totem creatures. Then there was silence. People began to lift their eyes from the ground. Was this all?

And then, deep down below the earth, they heard a strange rumbling, which grew and grew until the earth began to rock and shake. Great noises echoed from the Totem like the sounds of vast explosions in caverns deep, deep below the earth. The huge Totem pole shuddered and swayed from side to side. Then suddenly from its many mouths there came a great shrieking wind. It blew upon the camp fire and as it did so, it turned into great long tongues of flames . . . twenty or more fountains of fire spurting from the many mouths of the Totem!

And then David and Toby came racing across the camp towards Little Cloud and the old Chief, Bald Eagle, whom he was helping to his feet.

Laughing and shouting for joy they pranced round the bewildered Indians. 'Look, look!' they cried, pointing to the great tongues of flame. 'The Totem has spoken. The Totem has given you back your treasure, Little Cloud, Chief Bald Eagle—the Treasure of the Moccasins.'

Indians, cowboys and even the prisoners were now packed tight around them, watching in amazement. 'Oh dear,' cried David, 'can't you all see? Don't you understand? *It's gas from deep under the earth that's burning there—natural gas. The Moccasins are rich again . . . rich for ever.'*

Then it seemed that everyone began talking at once and laughing and shouting and cheering. Little Cloud stood before his father and put his hand on the shoulders of David and Toby. 'My brothers have brought us great fortune,' he said, 'and they must share our wealth. But there is something to be done at once, my father.'

'It is so,' said the old Chief. 'Hear me! From now on and forever these our brothers—they, their children and their children's children—shall be honoured as

Chiefs of the Moccasin tribe. Let smoke from every hill top send the news to all friendly tribes. Tomorrow there shall be a great feast to honour our new Chiefs.'

And as the cheering began again, the crowd was pushed aside and a great voice bellowed, 'Arrah, now, me bhoyos—what are we all waitin' for? Why not a bit o' song and dance to finish off this beautiful evenin'?'

And tucking his fiddle under his chin, Paddy Murphy began to play and sing a rousing Irish jig. But he could not have been prepared for the result. For at once all the Indians fell back. Little Cloud and Bald Eagle bowed their heads and flung an arm across their eyes. Paddy and his fiddle fell silent in bewilderment.

'It is the voice of the Totem!' cried the old Chief fearfully.

'The voice that set the Ugudugu-djuk to guard the wigwam of Hunter of the Moon,' added Little Cloud, remembering Mr Murphy's performance through the Totem pole.

David seized Paddy Murphy's arm. 'Now look what you've done!' he muttered. 'You've frightened them to death.'

'Yes,' snapped Toby. 'What are you going to do about it?'

Paddy Murphy was taken aback for a moment. 'Arrah, now,' he whispered, 'ye shall witness the rapididity with which me intellect dissolves a problem.'

Then he spoke in a loud voice. 'Hear me, Chief Bald Eagle,' he said. 'The voice of the Totem has spoken through me so that you may know you hear the truth. The spirit of the Ugudugu-djuk is imprisoned in this box that squeals. When the box is broken, then the Ugudugu-djuk will die and never trouble the Moccasins again. Behold!' cried Paddy. *'Behold.'* . . . and he waited for the Indians to open their eyes . . . *'I break the box!'* And with a great sweep of his arm, he smashed the fiddle down on the toe of his boot and shattered it to matchwood.

The happiness of the Moccasins was now complete

and Paddy was embarrassed by the thanks of the old Chief—and by the thanks of David and Toby too.

'I think that was jolly clever of you to think up an answer so quickly,' said David.

'Yes, and jolly noble, too,' added Toby, 'to break up your violin when it gives you so much pleasure.'

'I wish we could mend it for you, Paddy,' said David wistfully.

'Ah, well, no matter,' said Paddy, 'we made the old Chief happy and I reckon I did owe the Indians somethin' fer stealin' so many pairs o' moccasins and trousers from 'em.

'I suppose the poor ould fiddle's beyond repair,' he added, holding up the battered instrument and poking about inside it with his finger. 'Why, 'tis stuffed with paper in the corner here. Now, you wouldn't think that would improve the music, would you? 'Tis stuck down . . . come on now, come out with ye. Ah, here it is.' And he pulled out a piece of paper and held it close to his eyes. 'Would you believe it now, me bhoyos,' he exclaimed in astonishment, ' 'tis an envelope indeed, and with a name on it and an address.'

'Oh, Paddy, Paddy!' cried the boys, excited and exasperated all at once. 'What does it *say*? Who's it *addressed* to?'

Paddy scratched his ear. 'Well, it says here,' he said, holding the envelope sideways to catch the light from the camp fire, 'it says here, *"To my dear nephew"* . . . an' then underneath it says, *"Patrick . . . Aloysius . . . Demosthenes . . . Ignatius . . ."* '

'MURPHY!' said Paddy and David and Toby all together.

'Hurry up and open it!' cried Toby. 'Do hurry!'

Paddy stuck a big thumb under the flap and began to tear open the envelope. 'It must be from me Uncle Fergus,' he mused. 'Now I wonder why he hid the letter in me violin and what he wanted to say to me.'

110

CHAPTER 26

AFTER THE KILLER!

IT was hardly the place to discuss a mysterious letter written by an uncle of long ago, for Indians and cowboys were milling round excitedly, laughing, talking, singing and discussing loudly the Moccasins' newfound fortune as they watched the blazing geyser of natural gas spurting from the mouths of the Totem.

So David and Toby and Paddy Murphy slipped away to their ambush place and lit a fire. They huddled close together while Paddy held the letter near the flames and deciphered the crabbed and yellowed handwriting.

'It starts off,' said Paddy, ' *"My dear nephew, Paddy you young imp."* He was very fond of me,' explained Paddy. Then he read on: ' *"Many men go West to look for gold. But few men find it, Paddy. Now mark what I say, boy. I've had a Wise Woman lay a spell on this fiddle that I gave you. If your hopes of finding gold come to nothing then the fiddle will be broken and you'll find this letter. Take it straight to the bank manager back home in Ballysloggin. He has a copy and when he sees the two letters together, he will open my strong box and hand over all that is in it to you. There's your gold mine, Paddy—waiting for you back in ould Oireland. Sure, you'll be the richest man in the country. Uncle Fergus."*

'Well now,' breathed Paddy, overwhelmed, 'what d'ye think of *that*, me bhoyos?'

'It's wonderful,' said David, 'and you deserve it.'

'You must set off first thing in the morning for Ireland,' said Toby.

But, to the surprise of them both, Paddy shook his head.

'Ah no, I can't do that now,' he said.

'But why ever not?' asked David. 'There's nothing to stop you!'

'Listen,' answered Paddy. 'That gold's been sleepin'
in the bank there fer thirty or more years since me
Uncle Fergus died. It won't go bad if it waits a bit
longer. But I have a duty to your Uncle Septimus. He
did me the honour to make me one of Cobwebb's
Cowboys. I owe it to him to stay an' see this job
through by givin' me evidence against Spider an' these
prisoners here when they come up before the Judge.
That's me duty—and when it's done, me bhoyos, then
I'll feel free to claim me fortune.'

Now this set David thinking.

'You're right, Paddy,' he said. 'And that reminds me
that Toby and I have a job to finish before we start
going to any Indian celebrations. What do you think,
Toby?'

'You mean,' said Toby quickly, 'that we ought to be
trying to round up Jabez Gunn? I think it's our job, too.
After all, it was Paddy and us who unmasked the Big
O's plot and caught that man, Spider. I don't think this
adventure can really be ended until we've either brought
this villain Gunn to justice or—or—been k-killed in
the attempt.'

'Then I goes with you,' put in Paddy Murphy.

But David and Toby were determined to go ahead
on their own, and they persuaded Paddy that his job
was to remain on hand for the trial of the other bandits.

'I'm sure Lofty Cassidy can't spare any men to chase
Gunn until he's got all the others under lock and key,'
said David. 'We're going to set off tonight. You can tell
Lofty in the morning, Paddy.'

'I will, indeed,' said Paddy Murphy, 'an' 'tis a couple
of bold bhoyos ye are. But don't be over hasty. Take a
little while to think first. F'r instance, which direction
d'ye think Gunn would take? Why would he go that
way? That's what you've got to decide before you can
set off.'

Well David and Toby agreed that this made sense
and they sat and racked their brains and racked their
brains, while Paddy Murphy sat and pondered too.

After a long, long time the boys had to admit they

were not nearer a decision and they appealed to Paddy.

'Applyin' the machination av me intellect to the problem,' began Paddy, 'I consider he would make eastward across the hillside there and he would go on foot. On foot 'cos it's quicker among all them rocks than goin' on horseback, and eastward 'cos that's the quickest way to get to the Wailing River where it comes out from underground. If he can buy or steal a canoe from some fisherman, he could be miles and miles away even by noon tomorrow—faster than horses can travel an leavin' no tracks, mind. That,' said Paddy Murphy, 'is what me intellect suggests.'

The boys agreed that this seemed to be the only reasonable answer to the problem and Paddy led them stealthily round the camp. He brought them to the beginning of the trail over the hill and pointed out the route. As they were saying goodbye, Paddy suddenly exclaimed, 'but you've no revolvers! Here, take mine!' But the boys refused.

'You see,' said Toby, 'they're big and heavy and their weight will slow us up. And Jabez Gunn may have *his* revolver, but he has no bullets to shoot at us.'

'Don't worry about us, Paddy,' said David boldly. 'We'll get our man!'

And, as Paddy turned back down the hill, they melted into the shadows of the rocks.

CHAPTER 27

THE BED-POST EATER

THE hill was terribly steep, and the winding trail was dangerously strewn with loose stones. The shadows were black and weird and often masked great crevices that ran across the path.

Soon the boys were panting, but they kept on climbing doggedly. Slowly, painfully slowly, they began to come in sight of the ridge—black against clouds that were lit from behind by a watery moon. Suddenly Toby grabbed David's arm and pulled him to a stop.

'Look!' he gasped. 'Look there on the skyline! Somebody or something coming over the rocks towards us. Who is it?'

'Whoever it is,' said David, 'he's calling to us. Listen.'

Near as the figure was, the words seemed very faint.

'Something about a message, he says,' muttered David. Then, throwing caution to the winds, he called out, 'What do you say?'

The answer came clearly, but still faiint. And once again we shall have to put the words in very small type to show just how faint they were:

'I've got a message for you,' said the Giant Bat peevishly. 'Confound it, are you deaf? I'm shouting my head off!'

Although Toby had heard from David all about the Giant Bat, he still felt pretty scared when he saw it at close quarters, black and huge, with its glaring eyes, dripping fangs and the gleaming rows of steel claws along the edges of its great wings.

As they came to a halt before it, panting after the climb, the Bat said, 'As I was trying to tell you, I have a message for you. From Captain Cobwebb. Quote: I knew I could rely on you to see the job through. Good luck to you. Unquote,' said the Bat solemnly. 'I have to tell you that the man Gunn is far ahead of you. I saw him going into a house on the river bank. Over there . . .' and the Bat pointed a black wing across the rolling plain below. 'You can't possibly catch up with him now on foot. So Captain Cobwebb has sent that—that —that strange beast to help you. You'll find it waiting at the foot of the hill.'

'You mean Fanty!' gasped David.

'The elephorse,' Toby explained.

'If you mean the thing with four legs and a tail at each end, that's it,' answered the Bat. 'But I can't waste any more time. It's the Bat-postmen's annual meeting and they're waiting for me. In the belfry,' he added. And, spreading his wide wings, he swept silently into the clouds.

114

David and Toby lost no time in scrambling down to the bottom of the hill where Fanty greeted them with a squeal of pleasure and swung them in turn on to his back. In the far distance, the river glinted in the rays of the rising sun and they could dimly make out the small clump of trees that marked the position of the house that the Giant Bat had pointed out. Fanty set off towards it at a spanking pace while David and Toby chewed on lumps of rubbery pemmican—not to be compared with bacon and eggs and sausage but (as Toby said, with a deep sigh) better than nothing.

Soon they could see the wide expanse of the river, then the shape of the house—a tumbledown shack surrounded by a broken fence. Half out of the water beside the shack was the decaying hulk of an old paddle-wheel steamer. At least, the paddle-wheels could be seen but there was no sign of anything above the deck-line.

'That thing will never sail,' commented Toby, as they drew nearer.

'There may have been a canoe here,' said David. 'Gunn would have money in his pocket. He could afford to hire one, or even buy it.'

'Or just take it,' added Toby, 'if there was nobody in the house to stop him.'

But there *was* somebody in the tumbledown old shack, for, as they drew nearer, they heard a voice . . .

'Help!' cried the voice. 'Help! . . . Help!'

Fanty pounded up to the rickety gate and David and Toby flung themselves from the saddle and dashed through the open door into the shack. It was a strange sight that met their eyes. There, in a corner of the room, was an old man. He had his back towards them and his hands were tied behind him by a long coloured scarf.

But what brought the two boys to a halt was the fact that the old man appeared to be trying to chew one of the big brass balls at the end of an old-fashioned iron bedstead.

'What you waitin' fer?' roared the prisoner. 'Untie

115

me, get me out o' here. Let me get me hands on that hatchet-faced robber . . .!'

'That's Gunn's scarf,' commented Toby, as he whipped the bonds from the old man's wrists. But the victim continued to dance up and down, waving his arms, without moving from the spot.

'Come round the front!' yelled the old man. 'Come round the front of me and untie me face!'

And as David and Toby rushed to answer this strange request, they found that it was no wonder that the old man seemed to be biting the bed-post, for his long moustaches had been firmly knotted round it.

'Keep still, we'll cut you free,' said Toby, soothingly.

'No, no!' cried the victim. 'Don't cut 'em. I spent forty year a-growin' 'em. Untie 'em! Thet villain couldn't find no rope to tie me up so he done used me whiskers. If ever I lays hands on him, I'll . . .' But he had to stop there because both Toby and David were wrestling with the knot and he just couldn't speak. Finally they managed it and the old man twisted his whiskers lovingly till they stood out three feet on each side of his face.

'We know the man who tied you up,' said David. 'He's a murderer and we're chasing him. Did he hire a boat from you?'

'Hire a boat!' said the man indignantly. 'He *took* it . . . I found him jest a-gettin' into it an' tried to stop him. But he tied me up.'

'Have you got another boat that you can lend us, so that we can go after him?' asked Toby.

'If I had, I'd gladly give it to ye,' said the old man. 'But there's nothing else except the old hulk out there.'

'That broken-down old paddle steamer?' asked David. 'Will it float?'

'Oh, she'll float all right,' said its owner, 'but she's a great, heavy thing. Come out and hev a look at her . . .'

The old hulk was indeed so big and heavy that it would have been impossible to make any speed by just paddling it along. All they could hope to do was to drift down river and try to keep the boat straight.

116

'And I doubt ye'd catch up with thet robber,' said the old man, 'fer a canoe kin travel mighty fast and he's hours ahead of ye.'

David and Toby stepped into the hulk. There was nothing left of the machinery except the two paddle-wheels and the crankshaft with the two bends in it where the pistons had once fitted on to turn it round.

'Perhaps if we both get hold of the shaft we can manage to turn it,' said David. They huffed and they puffed and they strained . . . but it was no use, they just could not make the shaft turn even an inch.

And then, just as they were giving up, Fant's inquisitive trunk came between them, moved them gently aside, and the elephorse stepped daintily into the boat. Gently he twined his trunk round the shaft and pulled . . . and pulled . . . And, with a screech of rusty bearings, the great paddle-wheels began to turn, water formed white around them and the heavy old boat tugged at its mooring rope!

'Hurray for Fanty!' cried Toby.

'Is it all right if we take the boat, sir?' asked David.

'Take it and welcome,' said the old man. 'There's no need to bring it back. I'm moving away from these parts anyhow. Too dangerous, what with robbers,' he grumbled, 'and Trolls . . .'

'Trolls!!' said David and Toby in amazement.

'Yep,' said the old man. 'We druv 'em out once, but seems they may be comin' back. Two of 'em were here last night. They nipped at me toes while I was in bed and started questionin' me. They want vengeance agin someone. Cain't remember just what they said . . .'

At that moment the rotten old mooring rope snapped. Fanty turned the paddle-wheels lustily and the boat began to surge out into the river.

'Oh yeah,' called the old man, 'I remember me now. Them Trolls was askin' me if I'd seen two young boys around these parts. Say, it couldn't be you they was lookin' for, could it?'

CHAPTER 28

THE TERROR OF WAILING RIVER

BUT there was no time to think of Trolls for the man-hunt was on. The tireless Fanty made the paddle-wheels spin merrily on their creaking, rusty bearings. Toby gripped the spokes of the worn old steering wheel and David stood ready at the prow with a great pole to push aside any floating obstruction.

The river was broad and placid and the country flat on either side and they made good progress—but there was never a sign of Jabez Gunn and his canoe. Slowly the landscape changed, however. Rocks began to appear on either side and grew higher and higher. The river narrowed and flowed more swiftly. Fanty was able to rest, for the boat was now beginning to move faster than the paddle-wheels could drive her. The water foamed and hissed around great boulders that showed above the surface and David and Toby were constantly busy with pole and rudder to keep the heavy craft from smashing in her bows.

Then suddenly, as they swept crazily round a bend, David cried, 'Look—there's Gunn!' And they saw the bandit's canoe, a tiny spot far ahead of them, tossing and turning in the white foaming waters.

Slowly, slowly, they gained on the man until they could see him working desperately to keep his frail canoe on an even keel.

'If we catch up with him, what do we do then?' said Toby.

'There's only one thing I can think of,' answered David. 'We must try to force his canoe into the shallow water near the bank. Then, if he tries to run away, Fanty can leap out and grab him while we drive our boat aground. Then we'll tie him up and Fanty can

118

take us all back to Uncle Septimus at the Double C Ranch.'

By now the sunlight had left the gorge, the air was chill and the wild waters thundered around them. They were within hailing distance of the fugitive when suddenly they saw Jabez Gunn fling back his head and, with a shout of terror, begin furiously paddling to try to change direction. And at that moment, with a hideous shrieking sound, a huge boulder hurtled from the lip of the precipice above!

It hit the river within inches of the canoe, sending up a huge column of water that soared high, wavered, and fell on the fleeing desperado. It swamped the canoe and sent the paddle flying from Gunn's hand. Screaming with terror, he tried frantically to bale out the water with his hat while the canoe began to founder.

A sudden scream of anger from Fanty drew the boy's attention to their own danger . . . for already another huge rock was sweeping down on them. It missed the boat but, as the heavy craft rocked, David and Toby saw high above, on the edge of the cliff, yet another great boulder, teetering and ready to fall. And round it, and spread out along the lip of the ravine, was a line of little black figures . . . figures whose shape the boys knew well . . .

'Trolls!' cried David.

'Trolls!' shouted Toby, as the huge rock came screeching down.

But Fanty had moved swifty to dodge the danger and, straining, with legs wide apart, he set the paddle-wheels spinning. The sudden move was enough to take the boat just out of danger, but a great cloud of falling spray drifted like a curtain in front of them and they could not see where they were going.

As it cleared there was an agonised cry close to them.

'Help!' cried the voice of Jabez Gunn. 'Save me!'

He was struggling in the raging water, desperately trying to reach their boat. Ahead of them David had a quick glimpse of the canoe, as it floundered against a rock and was smashed to pieces.

'Grab the side of the boat,' David shouted to Gunn. Then, 'Steer for the shore, Toby.'

'Keep it up, Fanty!' yelled Toby encouragingly, as he swung the wheel over, and the elephorse, turning the wheels at top speed, drove the heavy craft across the current towards the shallows and the shore.

Fortune seemed to be with them, for here the cliffs fell back. There was a tiny bay of sand and pebbles, and behind it a narrow but steep valley that led up to the top of the cliffs.

With Jabez Gunn hanging on to the side of the boat, Toby steered until the prow grounded near the shore. Fanty turned and stretched down his trunk to reach the bandit.

But Jabez Gunn had his feet on firm ground and, ducking to avoid Fanty's trunk, he scrambled to the shore and began to run up the beach.

'He's trying to escape!' cried David. 'Quick, Fanty, after him!'

The elephorse, trumpeting fiercely, leaped from the boat, setting it rocking violently. But, as it reached firm ground . . .

'Look!' cried David. 'Look at Gunn . . . he's running back again!'

He was indeed running towards them, babbling in terror and casting terrified glances over his shoulder. And well he might! For seething down the valley, pouring like a black flood over rocks and boulders, came the Trolls—thousands of them, hissing and slithering on their scaly feet. The sound of their steely claws snapping together was like the rattle of a thousand kettle-drums.

But Fanty did not falter. His powerful trunk closed round Jabez Gunn's chest. He swept the struggling bandit from his feet, then half turned his head to see if David and Toby were following.

But the lightening of the great boat as Fanty leaped from it had set it afloat again and the thrust of his feet as the elephorse jumped for the shore had pushed the stern of the boat out into the current.

David and Toby, all set to jump, found their boat in deep water, turning dizzily as it was swept ever more swiftly into the surging waters.

'Fanty, Fanty, take him to Captain Cobwebb!' yelled David at the top of his voice.

'Never mind us!' screamed Toby. 'Take him to Captain Cobwebb . . . Captain Cobwebb!'

And the elephorse understood. As the black torrent of Trolls surged round his feet, great pincers stretched to nip his legs, Fanty trumpeted a wild note of defiance and advanced. Still holding the desperado round the chest, Fanty swung him to and fro like a great pendulum. The bandit's riding boots, with their long spurs, sliced a path through the Trolls as clean as if a great lawn-mower had been driven into them.

The last that David and Toby saw of them was Fanty, pausing triumphant, at the top of the cliffs, with Jabez Gunn held high above his head.

And, as the elephorse set off at a gallop to the Double C Ranch to deliver his prisoner, the high cliffs closed ever more tightly on the river, and David and Toby found their boat surging along at breath-taking speed. The air was filled with a hideous wailing noise that grew louder and louder, then . . .

'Look, David. Look there!' yelled Toby.

Right ahead of them was a huge rock face, blocking their path, and at the bottom of the precipice gaped a great black mouth. Into this mouth the entire river poured and from it came the weird wailing that made it seem like the entrance to a cavern of demons.

'Hold tight, Toby!' called David. 'Hold tight.'

'I am holding tight,' cried Toby. 'Oh, David, David . . . what's going to happen to us?'

And then, with a wild shriek, the Wailing River swept boys and boats into the blackness of the cavern.

CHAPTER 29

CORNERED BY THE TROLLS

INSIDE the tunnel the boat was swept along at great speed. Sometimes the water was so high that the sides scraped the roof, so David and Toby lay in the bottom of the boat and just hoped that it would not be submerged and that somewhere, sometime, the river would bring them out again from under the ground.

Meanwhile they tried to put together all the bits of information they had picked up about the river and its course and about the Trolls as well.

'I feel certain that the Wailing River has been a sort of highway for the Trolls,' said David. 'You remember there was a Troll colony in the mountain by the Moccasin camp. Then they were driven out. They must have gone down the river . . .'

'And made a new home in Troll Woods,' said Toby excitedly. 'Wailing River is supposed to go under the mountains that reach up to the Mist Curtain. When we escaped from the Trolls we went through the Mist Curtain on Fanty's back. Now we must be going back under the mountain.'

'And we may find the Trolls waiting for us when we come out at the other end,' said David. 'The Trolls that Paddy Murphy saw weren't looking for a new home in the Moccasin country—they were looking for us. Remember the old man who let us have the boat—he said the Trolls were asking about two boys. You know what I think, Toby?' added David. 'I think the Trolls that were left after your treacle-pudding explosion got together and vowed vengeance. And I think they've been hunting us ever since!'

'Well, let's hope that the ones we've just escaped from

are all there are,' said Toby. 'If they were to catch us again, we couldn't play another treacle-pudding trick on them. They'd kill us right away.'

'Haven't we anything we can use for weapons?' asked David.

They each knew quite well that they had nothing to defend themselves with but they went through their pockets just the same, as the boat swept silently on.

'Nothing,' said David at last. 'Not even a penknife or a piece of stick.'

'Nothing,' said Toby, delving deep into one pocket after another. 'Nothing . . . well, nothing except a handful of old . . .'

But David wasn't listening. 'Look!' he cried. 'Look at the lights.'

The speed of the river slackened suddenly. The tunnel widened. Ahead of them the boys now saw a vast low arch of rock. Beyond it a huge black pool seemed to reflect a whole sky full of stars.

'Of course, it'll be night now,' said Toby, 'and that's the time when Trolls will be about. Just look at the stars.'

But David had been studying the reflections carefully.

'Toby,' he said, 'you'd better be prepared for trouble. Those lights are not stars. They come from lamps.'

'Lamps?' said Toby, puzzled.

'*Troll lamps,*' whispered David.

And as he spoke, the heavy boat swung lazily out from under the arch into a huge, still pool. This lay in the bottom of a great bowl of rock in which rough benches had been carved all the way round, like the rows of seats in a great circus. Around the benches, crammed with shadowy figures, glimmered circle after circle of tiny lamps.

In silence the boat drifted to the centre of the pool and stopped.

And as it did so a sizzling and hissing of hatred, like the sudden boiling of a multitude of huge kettles, burst from a thousand Troll throats.

'Well,' said David grimly, 'I wonder how McGinty's goat would get out of *this*?'

'He'd need a lot of time to think,' said Toby. 'If only we can keep them at bay for a while, we *might* be able to work out a plan.' But he didn't sound at all hopeful.

'All right,' answered David. 'Look out! The Troll-king is getting up.'

The hissing died away to silence as the Trollking rose. He must have suffered badly in the treacle-pudding explosion, for his new hair was only half grown and he looked rather like one of those brushes that are used to clean teapot spouts.

'Ssso!' he hissed venomously. 'We have sssecured you at lasst! Kindly ssstep ashore, sssilly perssonss. We are going to kill you.'

'Come and get us!' answered David. ('I'm sure they can't swim,' he whispered to Toby.)

The Trollking wriggled angrily and snapped his huge claw.

'Then ssstay where you are and ssstarve,' he sizzled. 'You will sssoon be asssking for merccy.'

'That gives us a little time, anyway, Toby,' said David. 'Can you think of *anything* we can do to get out of here? Wait a minute . . . what was that you were telling me when we were in the tunnel? About something in your pocket?'

'Oh,' said Toby despondently, 'I hoped for a minute . . . but it's no use . . . You remember when Little Cloud was hurt and I found the Zoga leaf that sort of made us so light we just skimmed the ground when we walked?'

'Yes,' said David, 'but we ate that leaf.'

'I know,' replied Toby, 'but I took all the rest of the leaves there were on the bush and I still have a handful in my pocket. I thought perhaps they might be useful but of course they've all dried up now.'

'Do you think it's any use chewing some?' asked David.

'To make really sure that we get all the power out of them,' said Toby, 'I think we ought to make a brew of

124

them—you know, like you do with tea-leaves—and drink the lot.'

'When we had it before,' said David, 'we had only one leaf among three of us. Even if the ones you have are dried up, how can we be sure we wouldn't poison ourselves by using all of them at once?'

'We can't tell,' said Toby. 'The only thing we *can* be sure of is that the Trolls will kill us unless we can escape. We've got to take a chance, David.'

'We can hardly expect the Trolls to provide us with two cups and some boiling water,' said David gloomily, and they both fell silent. Then suddenly David muttered, 'I wonder . . . I wonder . . . How about this for a plan?' And after he had explained his idea, Toby said, 'Right. Let's try it.'

CHAPTER 30

THE LAST BATTLE

DAVID stood up in the boat.

'O Mighty Trollking,' he said, 'we do not want to die.'

'Sssssilly persssonss—you have no choicce!' hissed the Trollking.

But David went on, 'In exchange for our lives, we will give you something most secret and wonderful.'

The Trollking fizzled and sizzled with anger until his little face burned bright red and steam came up through his crown. 'No, no, NO!' he shrilled. 'Not another reccipe! No more tricksss with ssstuff like Treacle Trollpudding!'

'Please, please listen, kind Trollking,' put in Toby very weepily. 'This is a secret potion we stole from the Moccasin Indians.'

Now this was a very smart thing to say, because of course Trolls, being so untrustworthy, have a great respect for stealing and such-like wickedness.

125

The Trollking simmered down. 'Ssso?' he hissed.

'Yes, Your Majesty,' put in David. 'When you ambushed us, we were running away with this secret. We were going to sell it and make a fortune. But if you'll only let us go, we'll give it to you, really we will.'

'I sssee,' said the Trollking sarcastically. 'And what will thisss potion, thisss elixxir, do for me?'

'It will make you,' said David impressively, 'the biggest, the hairiest, the strongest and the cleverest Troll in the whole world.'

'Indeed! Now ssshow me thisss marvelousss ssstuff,' hissed the Trollking.

Toby pulled out a fistful of the dried Zoga leaves and held them out in his cupped hands.

'Make a brew of these magical leaves with boiling water,' said David, 'and drink it as hot as you can. At the very first sip the magic will begin to work.'

'I sssee,' said the Trollking softly. 'But you have no fire and no kettle in that boat. Ssso you will have to come to the shore and hand over thessse magical leavesss to me, won't you, ssso that I can put them to the tesst?'

'We'll bring them at once, Your Majesty,' said David, and he and Toby dipped their hands into the water and began to paddle the boat slowly to the shore. 'And when you have become the hairiest, strongest and cleverest Troll in the whole world, you will let us go, won't you?' he added.

'Oh, yesss. You will ccertainly go away,' sizzled the Trollking, turning to his bodyguard of Trollknights with an evil wink. 'Help thessse young persssonsss asshore, Trollknightsss. Take the magic leavesss, Trollchef, brew them in the Royal Teapot and bring back the potion in the Imperial Cup.'

While they waited, the Trollking kept dancing about on his great scaly claws, fizzling and sizzling with wicked merriment and digging the Trollknights in the ribs with his great claw.

At last wild hissing and fizzing broke out among the huge concourse of Trolls as the Trollchef returned

126

with a great steaming silver cup. The Trollking took the cup and raised it.

'And now, I have sssomething to tell *you*, O sssilly young persssonss,' he hissed. 'You are not going to poissson *me* with thisss drink, asss you planed. You are going to drink it yoursssselvesss. Seize them, Trollnightsss,' he shrilled, 'hold their nosssesss and make them drink the poissson! We will watch them die!'

'Well, Toby,' whispered David, 'one way or another, this is the end of the adventure.'

'We promised we'd see it through,' replied Toby, 'and we will.'

And then the Imperial Cup was pressed to the lips of each in turn and the hot potion poured down their throats. The ruse had been successful—they had tricked the Trolls into brewing the magic liquid for them and giving it to them to drink. Now what would happen? Was the brew too strong and would it kill them? . . . were the leaves too old and would nothing happen, in which case the Trolls would kill them? . . . or would the magic work more strongly than before?

They were not long in doubt. For suddenly David gave a great and joyous cry and Toby seized his brother's arm and cried out too. And to the terrified hisses of the horror-stricken Trolls, the two boys shot up into the air like rockets.

'It worked . . . it worked!' cried Toby.

'Look out!' whooped David suddenly. 'We're going down!'

And down they swooped . . . down, down . . . down among the Trolls, who fizzled and sizzled and hissed and slithered this way and that in panic as they saw two pairs of cowboy boots, complete with spurs, hurtling down on them from the sky.

'Up again!' cried David. 'Did you see the Trollking's face?'

'Down we go,' laughed Toby. 'Yes, I did. I kicked his crown right into the water.'

Up and down they went and each bounce seemed to take them higher and higher. Now the Trolls and the pool were left behind and they were bouncing among trees. A faint glow far behind them showed where the Mist Curtain lay.

But higher and higher still they bounced.

'Do you think we'll ever get down?' quavered Toby as they soared to the highest point yet. But all David could say was, 'Oh . . . Oh . . . . . . OOOOHHHH!!' as they began once more to plummet down . . . down, down . . . down into a huge black cloud . . . *and down . . . and down and . . . then there was something very, very soft that gently broke their fall. Something soft and warm and very comfortable—so comfortable and sleep-making.*

It was just about this moment that Mr and Mrs Green opened the door of David and Toby's bedroom in Dingle Down and peeped in.

'Sound asleep,' whispered Mrs Green. 'How right you were, my dear, to insist that they went to bed early!'

'Of course I was right,' answered Mr Green, as he closed the door. 'I know how to deal with boys. A good sleep is much better for them than dashing about all over the place playing games of Cowboys and Indians.'

Grown-ups do say the oddest things sometimes, don't they?